The Onset Of Love

The Onset Of Love

Kathirina Susanna Tati

PARTRIDGE

To order additional copies of this book, contact
Toll Free 800 101 2657 (Singapore)
Toll Free 1 800 81 7340 (Malaysia)
orders.singapore@partridgepublishing.com

www.partridgepublishing.com/singapore

Contents

Chapter 1

"Mikol, I am so happy!" Inai Ulis exclaimed, smiling. She went to sit near her husband. Her face beamed at him almost radiantly. She pulled her well-worn but much-loved sarong more tightly around her for comfort, covering her legs, which were bruised from walking through bamboo groves earlier that day. Her face shone with happiness, and yet there seemed to be a sadness etched deep inside her. Her worries showed in the wrinkles and care lines on her face, lines of joy and sorrow carved on a face that was fast losing the vitality of youth even though at the age of reaching to 40s she looks like 50s.

Earlier, Inai Ulis had gone to the hillocks behind her house to look for bamboo shoots and wild mushrooms. These were eaten as vegetables and went very well with the silvery, scaly fish her husband caught in the river which is located behind the house. A small river but that is the place where they normally do fishing or put their net to catch fish. In fact, fish, bamboo shoots, and mushrooms were a daily meal for them, being one of the easiest repasts to gather in their village.

"Why?" Mamai Mikol asked, frowning at his wife. He was rather surprised at her strange exuberance that morning. Bemused, he placed his bamboo musical instrument, the *tongkungon*, on his lap and stared at Inai Ulis. His hand strayed to his sparse moustache. He watched his smiling wife busily rubbing her teeth. He kept on staring at her. She looked like she was in love.

Huh, he thought.

He looked away and stared out into the greenery beyond, where tranquillity seemed to reign. The peace within him seemed to glow and to encompass the glory of nature in the trees, the waterfall beyond, and the green and blue of the distant mountains. He felt joy in everything that nature offered, including the gigantic glory of Mount Kinabalu, especially before mists shrouded it some mornings. Sometimes it seemed the mists were protecting the mountain with as much love and reverence as he had for it. Kinabalu, or Nabalu to him, was, after all, the final resting place of the soul of his people, the Dusuns.

"Why? What makes you so happy today?" he asked his wife after a few minutes, taking up his tongkungon and playing with its taut strings. He stared at Inai Ulis, his eyebrows raised in inquiry.

"Jenny said Laura has given birth to a baby girl! We have a granddaughter," Inai Ulis answered happily, smiling like a village maiden who has just been wooed by the man of her dreams. "We are grandparents at last, Mikol," she said, wiping the dried mud from her legs. Smiling, she took off her headdress and began to smooth it out, folding the well-worn piece of cloth on her lap.

She liked the old headdress. Even though it looked worn and should indeed be replaced with a new one, she was reluctant to let it go. The old piece of black cotton cloth had served her well, shielding her against the sun for many years.

Sighing, she folded her hands on her lap and looked away. Despite the happy news that Laura had birthed a child, she felt a sudden deep sadness, as if her heart would break. It was as if an old wound had opened.

"It would be nice if she lived near us. We could go and see our grandchild," she said. She looked away into the distance, at the gigantic pines and other trees swaying in the wind. Her thoughts wandered beyond the trees and the Crocker Range, settling on the peak of Kinabalu, which was bathed in the morning sun.

"I miss Laura, Mikol. I thank God we have a grandchild," she said softly, her voice full of joy. There was joy in her heart, and she was glad that her child was happy, but she missed her elder daughter. The smile stayed on her face, but Inai Ulis felt a little weary.

If Laura had given birth in the village, Inai Ulis would now be the busiest grandmother. She would be gathering herbs for the new mother and proudly taking care of her daughter and granddaughter. Her house would no longer be so quiet. It would be filled with the sounds of the new addition to the family. She smiled widely as she rubbed the bruises on her legs, as they had begun to itch.

"Hah! You forget. Laura is no longer our child!" Mikol suddenly bellowed, breaking into Inai Ulis's reverie and startling her.

She stared at her husband's face in consternation. It seemed he was still angry at their daughter and had not forgotten the previous matter or forgiven the girl.

"She is no longer our child. She disowned us. She turned her back on our religion, culture, and traditions," he snarled. "She is an ungrateful child!"

The joy and happiness faded away from Inai Ulis's face.

"Haven't you realised what she did to us? Think!" Mikol snapped, thumping his chest softly. His eyes brimmed with sadness, pain, and anger. Then he thumped the floor with his fist and let out a long sigh. He found it impossible to express his grief. "I am displeased." He began to massage his chest. He let out another long, deep sigh and wiped his face with his palms several times. His red-rimmed eyes teared up.

"A disobedient child," he growled, thinking about his eldest child who had chosen to leave the family home to pursue the whispers of her heart. "Hard-headed and stubborn!"

"Did you forget?" Mikol asked his wife harshly, staring into her face fiercely. "She is a disappointment to me! We are her parents. How dare she repay us by going off with that man from Malaya." He again massaged his chest, which hurt as if thousands of bamboo knives were slicing it. The hurt and disappointment that he felt was almost unbearable. He tried to think of ways to forgive his daughter and heal his sadness, but he could not find any. All he could think about was how his beloved daughter, whom he had brought up with so much affection and care, had betrayed him.

"I am still upset and disappointed. I still can't forgive that hard-headed child." He looked up at the framed photographs of his children, of him, and of his family mounted on the wall of his living room. "We loved them so much. We took care of them, and she repaid us with this. I am affronted ... hurt," he said, palm on his chest.

Inai Ulis bowed her head in silence. Deep inside, she felt exasperated, as she too had suffered and was hurt and disappointed with Laura. But her longing for her beloved child surmounted the anger, making whatever hurt she felt become somehow more bearable.

"Your children never learned from the story of Si Tanggang?" Mikol asked Inai Ulis harshly.

She was reminded of all the stories she'd told the children in the past. Most of the stories were about filial piety and encouraged the children always to listen to their elders. "Stop being so angry, Mikol. Raging about your disappointment won't do you any good. She is still our daughter." Inai Ulis tidied her hair into a bun. She was still sitting near her husband, who was picking the tongkungon nonchalantly. "You can't disown your own flesh and blood."

"Flesh and blood? You forget her selfish wilfulness. She left her old parents just because she wanted to follow her heart. Her choice. Children nowadays ... obstinate!" He added, "They never listen to their parents," his thoughts going to the daughter who hadn't listened to his advice. "Well, that's her choice," he spat, placing the tongkungon near the entrance door facing the living room. He stood and strode off, leaving his wife alone in the living room.

Inai Ulis sat listening to the dogs playing outside the house. The barks of the mother dog, Kopi – Laura's pet – could be heard above the yapping of her puppies. It almost seemed like the dog was giving her puppies a talking-to. *Even animals love their offspring,* Inai Ulis thought, dwelling on her husband's determination to hold onto his anger at his daughter. Her pain seemed to resurface from deep within. It boiled over into a deep longing to see her daughter again. Laura had been such an affectionate child, and now that she was a mother herself, Inai Ulis could only imagine how happy she must be.

Inai Ulis was a grandmother, and her husband Mikol a grandfather. What happiness and joy it could have been for them if not for the happenings that had led to the anger and rift between them.

Her eyes misted over, and then tears fell down her cheeks. She remembered giving birth to Laura. After the pain of childbirth and the joy of having her warm bundle of joy in her arms, the days of postnatal care set in. Her own mother had attended to her with such tenderness for forty-four days, feeding her herbal medicine so that she would regain her health.

She thought about Laura and wondered if anybody was taking care of her postnatal needs. There were traditions to be adhered to. Would Laura's mother-in-law take care of her as required? Would all the taboos after childbirth be avoided? That was important, as this was Laura's first child. Question upon question swept through Inai Ulis's mind. *If only Laura had had her baby at home, I could take care of her just as my mother took care of me when I gave birth to my first daughter,* she thought. A sob escaped her lips as tears cascaded down her aging cheeks. Mamai Mikol came back with a glass of water, walking direct to he and seated at Inai Ulis side. His face frown and looking straight at his wife face.

"Oh, stop that! Why are you still crying? Do you think she even remembers us?" Mamai Mikol's harsh voice interrupted her thoughts.

"Don't be so heartless, Mikol. She is still our child." She cried, wiping her tears with her headcloth.

"Serves her right! Let her know the reality of life. Serves her right," he retorted. He sat down, careful not to spill the cup of cold coffee he held in his hands. "If she thinks about us at all, why doesn't she tell us personally about having the baby?" he added. "Stubborn!"

It seemed that Mamai Mikol was repeating himself. He was really angry with his firstborn.

"I can't believe that she actually did that to us … a child that we brought up with love and good instructions. All the sacrifices we made for her. I hocked my land to finance her education," he grumbled.

He reached out for his tongkungon and held it absently. "We made sure she completed her education. She got her degree, got a good job. After all that, this is how she rewards us," he added, sadness and regret creeping into his voice.

Inai Ulis did not reply, but she knew he was right.

"Think about it, Ulis. What father would not be disappointed?" He sighed, and looked out the window to the mountains beyond. "If I had more than two children, I wouldn't mind so much. Maybe the others would bring joy to our existence," he said. "I want her to know how hurt I am. I want her to know how disappointed I am with everything she did."

Inai Ulis listened quietly.

"With all this disappointment and disillusionment I feel, do you think it is easy to welcome her back?" he asked, gritting his teeth.

Inai Ulis, who had been lost in her own thoughts, looked at him, startled.

Mamai Mikol said, "That's your daughter! Stubborn. Ungrateful brat!"

"She takes after you, doesn't she?" Inai Ulis snapped, pointing at him.

Anger suffused her being as she listened to her husband's ranting and his berating of Laura. She agreed that Laura's decision was hardly a pleasant one. It had hurt her badly too. However, she respected her daughter's decision to follow her heart in pursuit of her own happiness. It could not have been easy for Laura to take that decision, but she had to live her own life without her parents.

Still, in Inai Ulis's eyes, her daughter's choice was not right. Laura had chosen Shukri, a man not of their race and a stranger to their culture, traditions, and faith. If it had been otherwise, happiness and joy would have been theirs as a family, and their everyday life would have been serene and idyllic.

On the other hand, Inai Ulis believed that she and her husband were being unfair to Laura, as they had left her out of their lives, withholding their love and support. She felt that this was not right, even though she felt saddened about her daughter's choice.

"Oh, Laura, you are such a good child, so well-mannered. Why are you so obstinate? You left us to follow your emotions, your heart," she whispered, remembering her sobs and tears as her husband told Laura to leave their house. Laura had left with the parting remark that she would never bother her parents again.

That promise was held true, as Laura had never bothered them again, Inai Ulis thought, except for leaving them with heartbreak and pain.

She looked at Mamai Mikol, who seemed lost in his own thoughts. His tongkungon was by his side as he held a *seruling* (flute) in his hand. He sat against the bamboo wall with the old seruling, looking into the distance.

Inai Ulis knew her husband missed Laura tremendously. She also knew that he had done his best for their two daughters where education was concerned. In his own way, he had brought them up the best he knew how. She watched him as he raised the seruling to his lips and blew out a melody that seemed to mirror his feelings. The sound emanating from the bamboo instrument seemed to caress the cool air and wind its way into Inai Ulis's heart. The music seemed to speak of winds soughing through the treetops and reaching for the peak of the cool mountains beyond. As Mamai Mikol played the seruling, his eyes gazed into the distance.

He alternated his seruling music with the tongkungon, on which his fingers plucked a rhythm that invited dancing.

Inai Ulis observed his nimble fingers plucking out the music, but her mind was on Laura. She loved her daughter very much and missed her every day, even though she had been hurt by the young woman's decisions. As a mother, Inai Ulis regarded her love for her daughter as foremost. Any wrongdoings and faults were secondary.

Gazing at the broody Mount Kinabalu in the distance, she thought about the power of her daughter's love for her beloved, which had lent her the strength to leave her parents and all they represented to answer the call of her dreams.

Inai Ulis began singing softly, her fingers slowing folding the areca leaves, beginning to make the betel nut chew. As her fingers prepared the chew, she sang songs that she had sung for her daughters when they were babies. She seemed to travel back in time. Once again she was with her girls singing to them softly. Her heart seemed to swell. She thought about her love as a mother, love that was as deep as the sea and as high as the sky. Her tears cascaded down her cheeks as she closed her eyes. She swayed softly as she would when holding a child. And she sang: "Sleep, my darling child. Smile within your dreams. I sing this love song, song of pure love from above. Sleep, my darling child. Mother's love unending, protecting you from harm, shielding you from danger, ending all sadness. A love that heals your sorrow, bestowing happiness and joy. Sleep, my darling child."

Chapter 2

Tears streamed down Inai Ulis's face as she recalled how she had been both mother and father to her two children for five years. During the time when her marriage was going through some tribulations, the hardship she'd had to endure in bringing up her two very young daughters on her own, without any financial assistance or emotional support from their father or his family, was terrific.

As the memories hit her, she once again recalled heartbreaking episodes. She seemed to sink into the cold nights, the coldness hitting her to the very bone. During those years, it was as if her existence consisted of dark nights without the presence of stars or light from the silver moon.

"Where's your husband, Ulis? How long has he not been home?" Odu Madilin had asked one day.

She could not answer her mother-in-law, as she did not know how to tell her that her husband had not been home for the last two years. It had been that long since he had gotten a job as a security guard in a supermarket in Kota Kinabalu, leaving her and her two kids in a small village in Poring, Ranau which is about three hours' drive to Kota Kinabalu.

Of those two years, Mikol had not sent any money home to her for the last eight months. There had been no milk for the baby. Inai Ulis had had to feed her with sweetened water. She was not all that helpless, however, as she had planted rice and vegetables for their own sustenance. She had also caught fish in the river for their food. When there were surpluses, she would walk through the village to sell her wares. Since her children, Jenny and Laura, were still small at that time, she'd had to carry them around.

"Maybe he met another woman!" Odu Madilin stated.

Inai Ulis had remained silent, but deep inside, her heart broke and her chest felt so tight that it seemed about to implode. She felt the urge to scream and cry, but she did not want to break down in front of her mother-in-law.

"You should go to the city and look for your husband," Odu Madilin spat angrily, flinging her *siung* (conical headcover) onto the table. "Tell him to come home and resolve your problems. If he doesn't want to be with you anymore, then get a divorce!

"You are still young, Ulis. If he doesn't love you anymore, he should just let you go," the elderly lady added, her anger apparent in her tight lips.

The woman knotted her greying hair into a bun, pinning it in place with her *timbok* (hairpin). Her height and her demeanour belied a strong-willed woman who was not easily swayed.

"But, Mother, the city is huge. I don't know where he lives," Inai Ulis answered.

"So just wait," her mother-in-law retorted, striding to the window and spitting. The red colour of the areca nut she was chewing splattered on the ground below. "You are stupid!" she stated, turning to glare at her daughter-in-law.

Inai Ulis bowed against her mother's displeasure, as she knew she would not win an argument with the older woman. Odu Madilin had been well-known for her no-nonsense demeanour and austere ways during her five-year tenure as village head. She was well informed in the matter of traditional laws.

For some time after that day, Inai Ulis in vain waited for her husband to come home. The waiting was growing difficult for her.

At last she made a decision to look for him in the city. It had not been an easy choice for her to make; she'd had to dredge up all the strength within her to decide to venture out to look for him.

She started her endeavour by meeting Pakcik Wahab, a neighbour who was working as a labourer with the Sabah Sports Board. She would go with him to the city. She also made an arrangement to leave her two girls with her mother.

Her journey began that fateful morning with Pakcik Wahab, sitting at the passenger's seat, when she travelled towards the city thinking up various scenarios.

"Men forget so easily," she muttered, thinking of Mikol's promise to come home periodically and to send financial assistance to his small family in the village. Her children had been very young then.

Pakcik Wahab might have seen her expression and felt guilty, as he had been instrumental in helping Mikol to get the job in Kota Kinabalu, which had resulted in the domestic turbulence.

"Ulis, when we reach the city, you must not make a scene no matter what happens. Think rationally," Pakcik Wahab advised, interrupting her thoughts. "Don't embarrass your husband and yourself," he added.

He kept on speaking to her and imparting all manner of advice, which made Inai Ulis feel even more apprehensive, giving her the impression that something had happened and everything was not all right. Having an inkling of what might have happened to cause her husband to stop sending word home, she felt her heart constrict.

She kept on telling herself that she would be strong, ready for anything. She would take everything in her stride and not be swayed by jealousy or indignation. She could not lie and tell herself that she was ready to be a single mother, as she needed her husband to help her in bringing up their children. She needed financial and emotional support, as well as moral support, from him in order to do that. Also required was that he be there for her in future.

She recalled her mother-in-law saying, "If your husband had married another woman in the city, let him be. But he must return to the village and resolve the problem. Ask him to pay *sogit* [conciliatory fine]."

Upon reaching the city, Inai Ulis went to the supermarket that was Mikol's place of employment. She saw her husband having lunch with a younger lady. Whom introduced herself as Mamai Mikol's girl friend. She was stunned and devastated to find out that her husband was having a love affair with a woman who worked as a cleaner in the establishment.

"You should remember your family in the village before you have an affair with a woman here! What will your children eat? Stones?" Inai Ulis shouted at her husband.

Mamai Mikol didn't answer. Instead, he took out RM200 from his wallet and proffered it to Inai Ulis, who snatched it from his hands.

"Don't embarrass me in my workplace, Ulis," Mamai Mikol had stated, grabbing her arms and pulling her away from his station. Ulis pulled away from him and pushed him back. He fell against a wall.

"Don't ever return to the village! Just stay here!" she yelled, her tears falling fast down her face. She wanted to hit her husband badly, but there were onlookers. With great effort, she kept a relative calm, the money clutched in her hand.

"You think this money suffices?" she asked angrily, glaring at Mikol, who was now standing up and staring at her with a confused look on his face.

"Don't make a scene in my workplace," was all he could say.

Her rage boiled over. She felt like a discarded piece of old cloth.

"I want a divorce! Go back to the village to attend to that! How dare you, leisurely going around with another woman! Unfaithful!" she yelled, pointing her finger at his face. With all her strength, she slapped him.

"No wonder our children are always unwell! It's because of you … your infidelity!"

She walked away, leaving Mamai Mikol standing there too stunned to make a move or even react. She almost dragged her feet, as she felt weary and tired.

"Stop making a scene, Ulis. Let's go home," Pakcik Wahab said, approaching her and putting his hands on her shoulder.

On the way back to Ranau, leaving her husband stunned and confused, Inai Ulis broke her silence to Pakcik Wahab, saying, "If

I go with how I feel, I could beat him up and smash his face. I was counting the days for my husband to come home to us. But look at what he has done."

Her fury was like bubbling lava ready to erupt. She trembled, trying to control her anger.

She felt that she could kill somebody.

Pakcik Wahab, however, talked to her about the consequences of giving in to her anger, and soothed her with his views and thoughts. She calmed down after a while, focusing instead on her two girls, who were waiting for her in their grandmother's house.

What would happen to them if I went to prison for killing someone? she thought, which notion made her shiver.

She'd heard about situations in prison from her cousin Jerin, who was once imprisoned for stealing buffaloes five years ago. He had unwittingly joined a gang that specialised in stealing buffaloes wandering near the lonely village road. The gang's thievery skills were vanquished by the law. Some of the gang members, along with Jerin, served prison time. Jerin and his gang spend 24 months in the prison. Jerin had related some horrendous happenings within the prison walls.

"Just let the matter take its course. I will speak to him about returning to the village," Pakcik Wahab spoke, adding that it had not been right for Inai Ulis to make a scene in public. "Don't worry, Ulis. You are still young and attractive. If your husband is unfaithful, just ask for a divorce," the elderly man, who had never married, said.

"I know. It is easy to get a divorce. But I want my children to have the love of a father. I want them to be happy," she answered sadly.

She knew that she was still attractive to men, as many incidents had occurred to remind her that she was still a young woman. She could have embarked on an affair many times over if she'd had no respect for her marriage vow. She could have sidelined others for her own happiness, but she had persevered in protecting her family and marriage. Her children had been her foremost priority. She was ready to live in abject poverty just to make sure that the family she built with Mamai Mikol stayed intact.

"One day the children will understand," Pakcik Wahab said, interrupting her thoughts.

She looked away. She didn't have much of an academic education, but she had her own values and held on to her own integrity. It was within her rights to have her husband's love and support, but she would not wrangle for it.

Inai Ulis returned home to her routine. She tended the land for her and her daughters' sustenance. She made sure they had food to eat, a roof over their heads, and clothes to wear. There were the usual tribulations and challenges, but Inai Ulis was determined to surmount them – and she did.

Five years later, her life changed again. She did not know whether it was for the best, but she knew she had to face it with an open mind, if not for herself, then for her daughters.

Mamai Mikol, her husband who had been living with another woman for all those years, returned home. He seemed genuinely contrite.

"Ulis, forgive me please. I regret my past actions," he had begged, holding her hands.

She looked at him and thought about him being in the arms of another woman all that time. Happy with the other woman, he had forgotten his wife and daughters. He had promised to be faithful to Inai Ulis. She had respected him, but he had fallen for another woman. Those thoughts went round and round in Inai Ulis's head. She would have rejected Mamai Mikol if not for her daughters.

"I forgive you, but remember, don't ever repeat this mistake. If you do, I will leave," she said after a short silence.

To his credit, Mamai Mikol did try his best to regain Inai Ulis's trust and confidence in him. He tried to please her in the hope of recapturing her love and affection.

As for Inai Ulis, she forgave her husband, but she could not forget all the hurt and pain she'd had to endure because of his infidelity. She could not forget the loneliness she had gone through during his absence. On top of that, she had sacrificed her own needs for her daughters.

"You must pay the sogit to your wife and children," Odu Madilin later told Mamai Mikol.

"I am ready to do that, Mother, really. As long as Ulis forgives me and take me back," he said, while seated infront of his wife, looking appealingly up at Inai Ulis. Odu Madilin who is seated at the far end in the same living room just remain silent.

Inai Ulis kept quiet and just observed her husband agreeing with her mother-in-law. She was still resentful and angry, but she was accepting her husband back for her children, she thought.

"You must pay the conciliation fine of one live buffalo," the elderly woman stated. Mamai Mikol nodded. He then fed both his children and Inai Ulis a lick of salt each as a symbol of sogit, or appeasement.

After Mamai Mikol paid the fine and his wife and daughters went through the ceremony, he and Inai Ulis lived as husband and wife again. They tried hard to make their marriage work. Inai Ulis tried to forgive Mamai Mikol, and he tried to reconcile with her.

"I may be able to forgive you, but I will never forget the tales of what is now history. A sea of apologies washing my angst, a mountain of snow to cool the heat – but I will never forget. Though I may offer forgiveness, my trust is eroded. This sacrifice of mine, just for my beloved children." These thoughts played through Inai Ulis's mind during the conciliation ceremony, and they stayed with her for a long time afterwards. She had watched her relatives laugh and dance during the event, but she'd felt very removed. The buffalo had been slaughtered, food and drinks had flowed, and there had been general merriment. She tried to suppress her hurt and anger.

Chapter 3

Silence seemed to reign that dark night without the sparkle of stars on the velvet sky. The dogs broke the silence once in a while, with the female, Kopi, dominating the yaps and barks. Inai Ulis listened to the noises of the night, and once more she sighed with sadness as she thought about her daughter.

Laura had been a student at the University of Malaysia Sabah (UMS) then. She had a vivacious and friendly personality and made friends very easily. One of the friends whom she had brought home was called Shukri, a fellow student. The young man was from Johor.

"Mother, Father, this is Shukri. He is my college-mate in UMS," Laura had said, introducing the young man to her parents.

Mamai Mikol and Inai Ulis had been happy to accommodate their guest just as they had accommodated all of Laura's guests before. They showed him how the villagers lived, teaching him how to hunt and how to set traps. They had shown him how to shoot the bats that haunted their orchards at night. Since it was the month of May, a time to celebrate the end of harvest, he had accompanied the family to the village festivities. He had evoked laughter earlier when he ran screaming from the hillside with an armful of paddy stalks.

"Why is he running like devils are chasing him?" Inai Ulis had asked Laura.

"What's wrong?" Odu Madilin had asked in her turn, staring at an agitated Shukri.

"He is scared of leeches!" Laura had laughed, and everyone had rocked with laughter, while a pale Shukri responded with a wan smile.

Laura was scattering the paddy on a canvas sheet to dry before sending it on to the rice hut. At the same time, her father thrashed the sheaves. Later, Laura, Jenny, and Inai Ulis collected the straws and placed them in a heap to be burnt later.

Odu Madilin whistled for the wind as she winnowed the paddy. The empty husks flew as the good grains fell to the mat below.

The days went by. It was now time for Laura and Shukri to return to their college. Just two days before leaving, Shukri had boldly approached Laura's parents and asked them for Laura's hand in marriage.

After consulting Laura, it was concluded that she wanted the matrimonial union with the young man, much to her parents' despair.

"You can't marry a man who comes from so far away," said Mamai Mikol.

Shukri who is seated near to Laura at the living room, look down and holding Laura's hand. Laura gripped his hand softly and both of the look nervous. Mamai Mikol look at them fiercely. Inai Ulis who is also seated near them just look at his husband's face, looking confused and lost.

"You were both so kind to him, treating him like part of the family, but when he proposes to me, you start to hate him," cried Laura indignantly.

"We don't hate him, Laura. But you must think about it more so that you won't regret your decision in future. Don't hurry," said Inai Ulis.

"He comes from far away, Laura. How will we know whether he can take good care of you in future?" her father argued.

"How do you know if his family can accept you for what you are, a village girl?" asked Inai Ulis.

"Father, Mother, I don't think it's fair for you to say those things. It's not nice to jump to conclusions. Even though I have not yet met his parents, I know that they are decent people, as Shukri is well-mannered and loving," Laura said, looking at both her parents earnestly. "He comes from a family with good education and a solid financial background," she added.

"His wealth will not sway us," Inai Ulis had replied shortly. Laura bowed her head.

"But we love each other. He loves me," Laura had pleaded.

"Oh yes! Of course he loves you now, but wait until you have children. If he changes, then what will happen to you? You will have changed your faith then! You will suffer, believe me!" Inai Ulis argued.

"Marrying someone local here will not guarantee my happiness." Turning to glare at her father, Laura said, "You have disappointed my mother."

Both her parents stared at her. Mamai Mikol squirmed a little, remembering his own infidelity.

"At least if you are living near us we can still meet you and help when necessary," Mamai Mikol had answered.

*   *   *

"Crying and regrets are useless, Ulis!"

Inai Ulis was startled from her reminiscence by her husband's retort. She hadn't realised that she had zoned out for several minutes while thinking about what had transpired.

Remembering the event leading to their heartache brought back her ire, but her maternal instinct remained intact. She loved her eldest daughter no matter what had happened. Laura was a mother now, and that was what mattered to Inai Ulis.

Laura, you will always be my child, she thought.

She reached out for her betel nut and areca chew in her bronze container – her *salapa* – and, once she had it in her hand, began to the fold the areca leaves. She leaned against the wall and watched her husband playing with his musical instrument. The tune was one of lost love, entitled "Rumandawi". This famous tale was of a fairy maiden and her lover who went through the types of tribulations that all lovers in legends go through. He had lost her through his own indiscretion. Inai Ulis considered the lyrics:

> Magical Kinomulok,
> Woman of Utopia,
> A magical land,
> Adored by mortal man.
> Kudingking declared,
> "Our union could be worthy" –
> Both of similar realms;
> Both of Rumandawi –
> If you live, Kinomulok,
> And you hear my refrain
> Speaking of your beauty
> And your majesty.

Mamai Mikol's music stopped and he looked away. The sadness was apparent in his worn face. He missed his daughter, but he was also stubborn. He was not going to admit that he longed to see Laura.

Inai Ulis was just the opposite. All she could do was shed tears. She thought about the legend of Rumandawi and Kudingking. It was a sad story about a mortal falling in love with a woman from the magical realm. The man had gone against his vow, and in the end his wife returned to her land, never to return, leaving him in his own land.

As Kudingking longed for his wife, so was Mamai Mikol longing for his daughter.

You will come home someday, Laura, Inai Ulis thought.

Chapter 4

"When did your sister tell you that she had given birth, Jenny?" Inai Ulis asked her daughter.

Jenny brought a tray of coffee and boiled tapioca for her parents, and then she sat down to enjoy the fare with the elderly couple who are seated at the living room as usual.

"This morning, Mother. She had a daughter," she answered enthusiastically, pouring the coffee and handing her mother a cup.

Inai Ulis took the cup in silence.

"Is she well?" Mamai Mikol asked shortly.

"Oh, she is all right. Her mother-in-law is taking care of her," Jenny answered, dipping her tapioca in a bowl of grated young coconut and then taking a bite of it.

"That's good then. If she was nearer, we could pay a visit," Inai Ulis said, watching her husband's face closely for a reaction.

"We could go and visit though, Mother. I will complete my college soon. We could fly there," Jenny said, picking up crumbs from the floor.

"I don't know if your father would go," Inai Ulis answered.

"If he doesn't want to go, the two of us can go," Jenny said, wiping her fingers.

"We don't have the means to go, though. The fare to Kuala Lumpur is not cheap, Jenny," Inai Ulis answered.

Even if they had the money, surely Mamai Mikol would not be interested in going, as he was still furious with his daughter, Inai Ulis thought. Besides being so set in his ways, surely he would never agree to meet the daughter whom he had berated and even driven out from the family home.

Inai Ulis walked over to stand at the window. The night was cold. A gentle breeze blew against her face. The oncoming twilight lent a surreal quality to the surroundings, encouraging her melancholy to suffuse her being.

Laura will always be my beloved daughter, she thought, as her memories of what had transpired a couple of years ago assailed her.

After her husband had thrown their daughter out of their home, Laura sought shelter with Inai Ulis's cousin's daughter Sarah. Sarah had converted to Islam when she married a religious teacher at a school in the village.

"Get out! Just marry the man you want! Let Sarah arrange your wedding!" Mamai Mikol had shouted at Laura when she once again told them about her intention to marry Shukri. "Go! Get out! Don't ever shadow our door! Ever!" he had added, shoving Laura out through the door. He had torn his hands away from Laura's grasp as she was holding them, begging him for forgiveness.

Inai Ulis had taken the sobbing Laura into her arms and hugged her, saying softly, "Go, Laura. Follow your heart. You have made your choice. We can't stop you.

"Don't return when you are happy, Laura – only when in grief. I will always be here for you," she added. Then she let go of her daughter, her husband wrenching her away.

Standing there and looking at her daughter through cascading tears, she continued speaking. "Giving birth to you and taking care of you with love is our gift to you, which can't be valued in money. I just want to remind you that we are your parents and we will love you all our life, even if you no longer carry your father's name or adhere to our faith. Our ancestor's faith who believe that Kinoringan lived on top of the Mountain." Inai Ulis.

"Being a Pagan, we strongly believed that the mountain is sacred and our eternal place to rest when we die, so when you leave our belief, who will continue then," said Inai Ulis.

"What are you blathering for, Ulis?! Let her go!" Mamai Mikol yelled, shaking his wife's shoulders. "She is blinded by the man's wealth, so let her go! We are just poor village folks."

"You! Get out, leave! Don't come back! Don't even let us know when you get married. It has nothing to do with us!" he shouted, pushing Laura away roughly. She stumbled to the compound in front of the house, crying.

Mamai Mikol pulled Inai Ulis, who was crying disconsolately, into the house and then slammed the door. She cried harder as she listened to her daughter begging for forgiveness outside.

"I am sorry, Mother. Please forgive me. I love you!" Laura screamed from outside the house.

Inai Ulis kept on sobbing as she sat down, her back against the wall. The weather seemed to sympathise with her, as the wind had started to blow hard and howl through the treetops.

"It is all right, Ulis. Don't cry. She is not going anywhere, just to your cousin's place. Don't worry about her. She deserves it. We are her parents, but our wishes and opinions don't matter to her anymore. Stubborn child!"

Mamai Mikol sat down on the floor, his back to the door. He was furious with his daughter for choosing Shukri over her parents, but he was also sad about what had just happened.

Returning her thoughts to the present time, Inai Ulis mused, *Two years gone and Laura a mother now.* The sadness and despair she had felt back then still haunted her.

The youth of today have their own thoughts and opinions. They are not as we were; we listened to our parents. In the past, we never objected to our parents' decisions, she thought, remembering that a young man from the village had asked for Laura's hand in marriage once but was repudiated by the young woman.

The young man named Joseph, the son of the village headman, was dejected when his proposal was rejected, but Laura was firm in her decision.

"I don't want to marry Joseph, Mother. He drinks a lot," Laura had stated. The family respected her decision then. Inai Ulis wondered if perhaps Laura was already in love with Shukri at that time.

Inai Ulis walked to her bedroom and wearily lay down. She cannot continue talking to Jenny, it really hurts to think of Laura. Whenever she looks at Jenny's face, she thinks of Laura, how she missed her oldest daughter. But deep in her heart she still happy because Jenny is an obedient daughter who still stay with them in the house taking care of both of them.

Outside, Mamai Mikol's music still caressed the night air, plaintive in its rendition. She looked up at the rafters of their house as the cockerels started to crow to welcome the coming dawn. She closed her eyes and hoped for sleep, and yet it eluded her like a jilted lover.

Her thoughts flew to Laura again, wondering if her daughter had adhered to traditional postnatal practices.

Chapter 5

"Mother, Laura wants to talk to you," Jenny said, handing her mobile phone to Inai Ulis. Inai Ulis took the telephone with joy, but she was apprehensive. Slowly she rose up from her seat and walk to answer the call.

"Mother? It's Laura," her daughter spoke. She sounded very distant on the phone.

Inai Ulis listened to her beloved daughter's voice, the voice that she hadn't heard for the last two years. She wanted so much to say something, but nothing came out of her mouth. She opened her mouth to speak, but her lips merely trembled. Her hands seemed to sympathise, as they too started to shake.

"Mother? Are you there?" Laura asked.

Jenny took the phone from her mother's hand and hugged the elderly lady.

"Hi, Sis. Call back later, okay? Mother is not very well," Jenny spoke to her sister.

"Tell Mother I love her," said Laura. Then she hung up.

"Why didn't you say anything, Mother?" Jenny asked, still hugging Inai Ulis gently.

"Don't grieve too much, Mother, or you might fall sick again. I won't disappoint you as my sister did. Find it in your heart to forgive her," she said, wiping her mother's tears.

Inai Ulis hugged Jenny back and caressed her hair. She could not say anything, but she had choked when she heard Laura calling her "Mother". Her heart had overflowed with a great deal of love and longing for her eldest child.

"You are a good girl, Jenny, but I don't want you to be unhappy just because you want to please us," Inai Ulis said gently.

"Mother, I believe that happiness comes with our parents' blessings," Jenny answered, looking into her mother's eyes.

"I remember how you suffered in those years when Father didn't return home. I saw you struggle to bring us up," Jenny added, thinking of all the hardship they had gone through during those times.

There had been no financial aid from her father, as he was then living with another woman in the city. She remembered how her mother used to work all day to eke out a living, giving all her spare attention to her daughters.

The villagers had not been kind, gossiping about Inai Ulis being on her own and working outside the home in order to earn a living.

Inai Ulis's mother-in-law, influenced by the villagers, had called on her one day and scolded the younger woman for leaving her children at home.

"Your husband goes to the city to work and support you, but you keep on going out of the house for some reason. Are you meeting other men?" the older woman had said sarcastically on one occasion.

Needless to say, Inai Ulis was indignant. She retorted that she went out to work, not to meander around, as stated by the villagers.

"Work? When your husband is away, you go out and play?" The derision in the older woman's voice was apparent.

Inai Ulis lost her temper. She yelled, "If I don't go out to work, who will support me and my schoolgoing children? Do you think Mikol sends us any money? No, he doesn't, Mother! He is living with another woman in the city!

"Where are you when we need you, Mother? Do you think your son is an angel?" she continued.

Her mother-in-law went into a rage and slapped Inai Ulis hard on her face. She continued hitting her daughter-in-law until the latter fell to the floor.

Inai Ulis could easily have hit back at her mother-in-law, but she did not want to hurt the old woman.

Jenny's eyes overflowed as she remembered the event that happen infront of their wooden house and she was just 10 years old at the time. She hugged her mother, and in her heart she swore that she would never hurt her. She hoped to get married one day. She prayed that when she did, it would be with her parents' blessing. The only way that she could ensure this was to marry someone of the same religious, traditional, and cultural background as her family.

She inwardly winced as she remembered her relationship with a man from Kota Belud by the name of Harris. A lecturer in another college, he liked her a lot and had proposed to her. She had said no, much to his disappointment. Although she liked him too and something could have resulted from the friendship, she could not risk upsetting her parents as Laura had. She was saddened by the break-up with Harris, but she bore it bravely for her parents' sake.

"If you followed Laura's example, it would kill me, Jenny," Inai Ulis murmured, breaking into Jenny's reverie.

Jenny continued thinking. "My happiness. My parents' happiness. I don't wish to see any more tears on their cheeks. I don't want to see the marks of suffering on their faces. Let my love be buried on the side of Mount Kinabalu. Let my spirit be as firm as the mountain. Let my steadfastness bring joyfulness to my parents. My happiness is dead. With their tears, I will not be at peace. If they are filled with sorrow, I will not regret it if my beloved leaves with a broken heart. My love for my parents is more than everything in this world."

Jenny sighed deeply with sadness as she thought of Harris, but she knew that she couldn't have carried on loving him if she wanted her parents to be happy. She had repudiated Harris's love for her parents' sake.

She recalled her grandmother Odu Madilin telling her that hurting the feelings of her parents was a sin. Jenny personally hated to see her mother cry or to see any sadness in her father's eyes.

I'm so sorry, Harris. No love blooms in this heart. Let it all end here, she thought, simultaneously thinking of her elder sister. She understood that Laura missed home and the beauty of nature that surrounds her village. Jenny knew that her sister regretted having gone against her parents' wishes. She looked out of the window to stare at the brooding mountain before her and sighed. The gigantic mountain stood proud like a sentinel over the region, home to the souls of her ancestors.

If only the spirits of Kinabalu hear our prayers and God sees our situation, she thought, considering of all the stories and legends associated with the mountain. "I pray to God that he will grant peace and happiness to my parents. With peace, let them forgive my sister for her wrongdoing," she whispered.

Chapter 6

The remembrance of the years past was still very fresh in Inai Ulis's mind.

"Ulis, Laura will be getting married at the end of the month. The ceremony will be held at my house," Sarah had told her that fateful day. Sarah came to her house announcing that her daughter Laura will proceed with marrying the man of her choice. Shukri. Despite her parent's objection. Sarah, her cousin stayed at another village which can be reach in 30 minutes by walking. She came all the way walking alone just to inform Inai Ulis about her daughter and at the same time inviting them to attend the marriage ceremony.

"She is now taking religious instructions," Sarah had continued gleefully as if to stress the facts to Inai Ulis, who looked at her silently.

Inai Ulis felt her heart contract with a very physical pain, but she kept calm and collected. "That's good, Sarah. You organise the event. We will not interfere. After all, we don't even know what traditions you will adhere to," she answered.

"Oh, don't fret too much. It's your daughter's choice. Just let her and Shukri be. Children don't always listen to our advice," Sarah answered, holding Inai Ulis's hands. Both of them standing in front of the door.

"True. Easy for you to say, Sarah. You don't know how we, her parents who loved and nurtured her, feel," Inai Ulis replied, pulling her hands away from Sarah's grasp.

"I know what you mean. I am not in favour of such a situation either, as it affects our harmonious existence," Sarah said.

"But it's an individual's choice. I have gone through the same thing," she added.

Inai Ulis stared at her cousin and thought of the scandalous event in the past when Sarah had fallen in love with a young religious teacher who worked at the village school. Sarah had decided to marry Ustad Naim in spite of all the protests of her relatives. The difference was that her parents had passed away a long time ago in a road accident. There was no one there to hurt or disappoint. Her grandmother who had brought her up did not protest much as she loved Sarah and only wanted to see her granddaughter happily married to the man she loved.

"Do you remember how the villagers disliked me and bad-mouthed me at that time?" Sarah asked, breaking into Inai Ulis's reverie.

"I know. I remember it well. That's why I don't want my daughter to follow in your footsteps," Inai Ulis remarked, scowling at her cousin. She added, "I love Laura, Sarah, but Mikol is disappointed, as you can imagine."

After a moment of silence, she said to Sarah, "Your husband was sent here to teach, so you are still here. Other women who marry these foreigners go away with their husbands to their home state, and then some of them find out that their husbands are involved in polygamy. They discover that they are second wives, among other wives. I don't want Laura to have the same fate."

"Whoever you marry doesn't make a difference. Even those who marry locally are not so lucky. You nearly succumbed to that pitfall yourself. Mikol comes from this village and is distantly related to us, but he blundered too," Sarah stressed, driving the point home almost ruthlessly.

Sarah carried on gently as if to nullify the harshness of her words. "Ulis, whatever religion we practise, or whatever our ethnic background, we are all the same. We want love and happiness."

"All right, Sarah. You don't need to go into history, which will only make me crazy. Whatever it is, we are not giving our blessing to Laura's marriage," Inai Ulis retorted.

"Ulis, don't you have a little compassion in you for Laura's predicament?" Sarah asked, staring at Inai Ulis. Sarah was 5 years younger than Inai Ulis and she remembered how close they are during their younger days, during their teenage days.

"Compassion? Ask Laura that," Inai Ulis answered. "I gave birth to her, brought her up, and gave her an education! Don't you remember how I struggled for several years to bring up the two of them alone? I was mother and father rolled into one, Sarah. Don't you think Mamai Mikol and I have not done enough for her? Why then is she rewarding us with disobedience?"

Inai Ulis broke down in tears, her shoulders shuddering with emotion.

Sarah enveloped her in her arms. For a moment, the two women embraced in silence.

"Ulis, let her make her choice in her bid for happiness. As you know, we can't be with our children until death. They have a right to their own happiness. Whatever happens, the wedding is going to go through. Laura and Shukri want your blessing," Sarah said, breaking the silence.

"I don't know, Sarah. I am still reluctant to let her go. And Mikol is determined not to," Inai Ulis replied, pulling away from her cousin. "Let the wedding go on. Mikol and I will yield to Laura's decision. Sarah, as I said before, you take care of the wedding. We don't want to be involved. We will listen to the merriment from afar," Inai Ulis said sadly.

"Just tell her to remember that she doesn't need to come to us in times of joy and happiness, but that if she should fall upon hard times, she may come home to us. We will always be here. Tell her she has relatives at the foot of this great mountain."

Inai Ulis was so overwhelmed with her sense of loss that she started to sob. Tears cascaded down her face.

"Shukri and Laura actually want to meet you," Sarah said, breaking into her cousin's state of sorrow.

"No! Don't allow them to come here. There is enough discomfort and grief here. Don't provoke more. Don't come to this house even if we are in the throes of death!" Inai Ulis cried.

Sarah was taken aback.

"I am sorry you feel that way, Ulis. I hope you are not angry with me and my husband, just because we want to carry out our responsibility," she said.

Inai Ulis smiled through her tears. "We are actually grateful to you, Sarah, for taking up this responsibility. Go home, Sarah. Tell Laura we will no longer try to stop her. She has chosen her path. We will not be around for the marriage, as we plan to go away to the next village on that day."

Sarah prepared to take her leave. "Remember, Ulis, she will always be your child," she said just before leaving the house.

Inai Ulis stood at the window and watched through her tears as Sarah walked into the distance. *Laura is my child. As if I need reminding,* she thought, her memories sliding through the past to happier times when her children were growing up. She heard their {laughter again and recalled all the cuteness that little children exude. She flashed back to the time when Laura left the house after Mamai Mikol had thrown her out. She heard again her daughter's cries and calls for forgiveness.

She imagined Laura practising a religion that was totally different from her ancient belief, where priestesses and the departed were in communication in the various levels of the netherworld. Even the best of these priestesses would not be able to communicate with her soul for Laura when she died.

She sat alone for a long time, looking away in the distance. The house was quiet, as Mamai Mikol had gone into the jungle to look at the traps he had set two days before. Inai Ulis tried to imagine Laura's wedding and how it would be for Laura and Shukri. Then she thought of her own wedding with Mamai Mikol.

In retrospect, her own wedding was in accordance with her ethnic custom. The ceremony, according to her Bunduliwan (Dusun) roots, was colourful and very merry.

iIn a small village in Poring, where she came from, it had started with her being dressed in her traditional costume of black velvet and gold. Her friends and family were around her, even as her hair was twisted into a bun and held up with hairpins.

All bedecked in her wedding finery, she peeped out of the window when she heard the beating of the gongs in the distance, waiting to see her future husband approaching with a group of young men.

All dressed up in black velvet with gold trimmings, Mikol had looked handsome in his headgear, just like a warrior of old. Besides the band of merry young men, elders accompanied him, bringing the dowry.

His arrival was announced not only by the beating of the gong but also by the *pangkis* (war cries) of his group. There was a surreal feel to the whole scene, as it was a throwback to the ancient ways.

The presentation of the dowry was carried out in a ceremony, over which the village headman and security chief had presided, accompanied by Ulis's and Mikol's parents. A priestess was also present. Upon the completion of the handing over of the dowry and other items, the bride and bridegroom met and exchanged their vows in the presence of the priestess.

The exchange of balled rice was then carried out. To Inai Ulis, this was the vow of undertaking, the man promising to support the woman and their offspring in future, and the woman promising to support the man in his endeavours and to take care of the family.

After that, Ulis and Mikol had danced the *sumazau* together for the first time. He raised his arms like an eagle to depict his strength as he faced and circled her, while she raised her arms a little lower, as if dependent on his might to shield her from worldly harm and tribulations.

The melodious gong sounded throughout the day, as well as the *kulintangan*. The young and the elderly danced together in joy and merriment. Potent traditional wine, as well as other beverages, flowed, and the array of food was mind-boggling.

Three days after the wedding, the leaving-home ceremony was carried out. The groom took his bride home to his village and his house. Seeing the group of people walking into another village was always a great source of excitement; as such, the villagers always came out to watch.

Upon reaching her groom's house, Ulis had walked up the stairs, after first stepping on a rock sited on the compound. This was the symbol of firmness, indicating that the marriage would stay solid until the end of the couple's life.

Bride and groom each wore their conical hat to insure them against any evil or bad luck that might befall them in their married life. With the intricately woven rattan *sirung* on each on their head, they went through yet another ceremony, with the priestess chanting mantras of blessings for the couple and appeasement to malicious spirits.

Inai Ulis was saddened that Laura would never know what it was like to be married within her own culture and undergo the beautiful and symbolic ceremonies that had been practised for a very long time. Laura would never know the excitement of the days leading up to the wedding ceremony, when the slaughter of a buffalo would occur, or experience the seven days of merrymaking usually practised by her people.

Inai Ulis thought of Laura's choice of husband with distaste, a Malay man who could never understand her culture. The difference in their backgrounds was tremendous.

She heard a noise at the veranda and looked to see Mamai Mikol sitting on it, slapping dirt off his pants cuff.

"Mikol, Sarah came earlier to inform us that Laura's wedding will be carried out in a month's time after she embraces her new religion," she said apprehensively, as she didn't relish the idea of seeing her husband angry again.

"Okay! Let her get married. Why bother?" he answered her shortly.

She looked away, relieved that he had not started ranting again. She dwelled in her own disappointment and wished for the thousandth time that things would be different. Deep inside she prayed, in fact calling out to the Supreme God and the deities of Kinabalu to forgive the sins of her daughter.

Chapter 7

A few days after Shukri had asked for Laura's hand in marriage, he and his new fiancée were back in Sabah. "It's sad that we don't have blessings from your parents," Shukri said, his palms on his face. He was confused about Laura's parents' reluctance to bless the wedding.

"We are getting married. You are marrying me, not marrying them," Laura answered, touching his broad shoulder, both of them standing near to each other.

"I don't want it to be like this, I want your parents to accept me as I am," he answered, staring into her eyes. "I want to marry you, but I don't want it to seem like I am taking you away. I don't want you to have to sever your ties with them."

"We must not give up, Shukri," Laura said, holding his hands.

Shukri smiled at Laura. Collecting his schoolbooks from Laura's desk, he took his leave. Laura watched him, a little peeved at his attitude.

Shukri went to his motorcycle, mounted it, and rode home, his thoughts on Laura and their difficulty because of her parents' attitude.

Upon reaching his rented home, he walked in and sat heavily on the sofa. His books fell at his feet unheeded.

His housemate, Firdaus, came out of his room and sat near Shukri, looking a little puzzled by his friend's sighs.

"What's the problem, Shukri? You looked troubled," he said.

"I am worried, Fir. I really am," Shukri answered, taking off his helmet and putting it on the side table.

"Why? You failed your final exams?" Firdaus asked.

Shukri stared at him.

"Come on, tell me. Who knows, I may be of help. Unless it's about money, of course. That, I can't do anything about," Firdaus said, chuckling.

Shukri sighed and warded off Firdaus's playful jabs at his ribs.

"Fir, I am worried. Why don't Laura's parents like me? They don't want to meet me again, and they don't want Laura to embrace our religion. They want Laura to have a partner from their own ethnic background," he shared, almost as if talking to himself. He felt a headache coming on, which was further egged on by the sounds of racing motorcyclists outside the flat. He clutched his head in frustration.

"Shukri, that's tough, man. But you should just keep an amicable relationship with them," Firdaus said. "After all, after marrying Laura, you will move back to Kuala Lumpur, which is far enough. They can't do anything to you there," he added, chuckling.

"I can't do that. That's not me. I want to have harmonious relationships between my family and hers. I want to be accepted for what I am," Shukri answered, looking at Firdaus a little contemptuously. "I love Laura and I don't want to lose her. But I don't want her to forget her family. That's definitely not me."

His thoughts travelled to happier days when he was accepted into the family as Laura's friend. He enjoyed the easy camaraderie among the people. He admired the beautiful women of her tribe. During one of his visits, he had attended a harvest festival and was impressed with how friendly the people were. He also saw how they adhered to their customs and traditions.

His love for Laura deepened then, and with that came his wish to have her in his life as his bride. This had pushed him to ask her father for her hand in marriage, as was customary in his culture. He hadn't expected the answer to be in the negative, though.

Laura's father had been polite but firm when he said, "No, we don't want Laura to marry you." The words seemed to cut into his very soul.

He remembered how he had felt tremendously disappointed. His world seemed to grow smaller, constricting his very life.

Shukri knew that Laura loved him very much and would do anything for him. He, however, had his own principle to heed on the matter, as instilled by his upbringing, namely that he should not hurt others or cause them harm and discontentment. Still, he didn't want to make a decision that would come back to haunt him in future.

His late father had recited from the Quran, ar-Rum 21: "And of His signs is that He created for you from yourselves mates that you may find tranquillity in them; and He placed between you affection and mercy. Indeed in that are signs for a people who give thought."

His late father used to say this after they had their dinner and gathering with all the family, as his father wants all of them to be wise and humble.

His father had been very fond of reciting from the Holy Book to stress points he made to Shukri when the boy was growing up.

"When I marry Laura, I want to give her all of me, my love and affection, but would it be enough if she were still at loggerheads with her parents?" he said to Firdaus. "Eloping is not allowed in Islam," he added.

"Why? Laura wants to do that?" Firdaus asked, curious.

"No, things are not yet that bad. But she will if her parents keep on refusing to give their consent."

"Hmm, I am not into marriage laws. Anyway, that's a problem you will have to solve. I am sure you know what you are doing," Firdaus said, losing interest in Shukri's predicament and shifting his attention to the television program.

Shukri, smiling at his friend's short attention span, began to think of the past, when he first went to Laura's village.

In one of his many conversations with Laura, she had talked about the villagers' attitude regarding intermarriage with people from Peninsular Malaysia. They were opposed to it.

He had been intrigued by the story and asked why the people of Kinabalu, on the island of Borneo, east of the peninsula, held this view.

Laura was not sure why. Her answer had not been satisfactory to him.

"Maybe in those days, those from Peninsular Malaysia did not respect our culture and traditions," she had stated, looking at him with her dark eyes.

Shukri had stared into her eyes and at her face, admiring her natural beauty and her smooth skin. Her face was oval, a little on the round side, and exuded an inner beauty through her expressive eyes, which showed compassion, love, and affection.

Shukri admired her tenacity as she walked down the hills with sacks of paddy on her back, her small dainty feet stepping confidently on the worn path. He thought of her as a future engineer and once again admired her humble demeanour. To him, her character was impeccable and her femininity was adorable. She was a well-rounded woman.

My beloved, a future engineer but so modest and diligent, he thought, watching her.

Later during dinner, he had been delighted with the food served, especially the fragrant rice. He had commented on how good it tasted.

"Of course. We plant the paddy from good seeds," Laura's father had answered, smiling at him benevolently.

Shukri had looked at Laura. She had smiled at him, making his heart trip a little. How he loved her.

His memories moved closer to the present. He recalled the words that had become thorns in his heart and a hurdle to his dream of marrying Laura.

"You are from far away," Mamai Mikol had said. "If Laura marries you, you will move away. How do we know you will take good care of her?"

"I mean well. I love Laura and I will take care of her always," Shukri had said emphatically.

"No. We don't want to lose our daughter. We are not prepared to see our daughter leave our traditions and belief," Laura's mother had stated firmly, looking straight into Shukri's eyes.

"You can be friends. Give yourself time to think properly. You might meet another woman in future and thereby upset my daughter. Anyway, you are still studying. How will you support a family?" Inai Ulis said.

Laura had listened to the exchange very quietly. Her tears began to fall as her parents stated the obvious.

Shukri was jolted out of his reverie when Firdaus, who had grown tired of surfing the TV channels, slapped his shoulder.

"Come off it, Shuk. You worry me. Look at your face. Your scowl might become permanent. You look tired. Come on, Shuk, snap out of it. If she is meant to be yours, she will be," he said.

"I am not interfering into your affairs, Shuk. I am just concerned that you might fail your final exams. You know how important that is to your future. We came here to get an education, but with you it's something else."

"I know that, Fir. I am sure I can handle it," Shukri said, looking at Firdaus and smiling thinly. "Anyway, I am going home during our semester break. I miss my mother. Who knows, if I go home, a miracle might happen," he added.

Firdaus laughed and turned away to watch more TV, quipping, "Yes, do that. Stop worrying or you might not graduate."

Shukri smiled at his friend and vowed to himself that he would bring back home, a graduation scroll no matter what.

*   *   *

The road to Bandar Muar was straight and did not offer much scenery to interest Shukri. Instead, he thought about Kota Kinabalu. He wished that it were just down the road. He missed that city, and most of all he missed Laura. He wanted to embrace her and feel her warmth in his arms. He wanted to see her face framed by her long hair and smell her Elizabeth Arden perfume. Thinking about the time when he had fallen in love with her, he smiled. He thought that it was love at first sight.

Firdaus had laughed at him when he told him about his feelings.

"There is no such thing as love at first sight. If you say you are attracted, I believe you, but love? No. And you? You are always so distant with women; you are so picky. Love at first sight – hah!" Firdaus had said, laughing his high, and at times irritating, cackle.

"How would you know? You are the veritable Casanova," Shukri had answered, a little peeved with his roommate.

He had been in love before and, in fact, would have been a happily married man at the time if not for certain circumstances. He remembered his ex-fiancée, Sharifah, who had broken his heart and made him distrustful of women in general.

His beautiful former fiancée, Sharifah, had given him an ultimatum. It was either settle down and marry her or further his studies.

To ensure that they had a future together, she had offered him a position in her father's law firm. He was not too keen on working under his future father-in-law, as he wanted to make it on his own after completing his studies. That way he would not be indebted to Sharifah's father for the rest of his life. Having been accepted to further his studies at University of Malaysia Sabah, he did not want to miss out on this chance to acquire more education.

The beautiful and opinionated Sharifah, however, did not see things the way Shukri did. To her, his desire not to work in the law firm was a direct confrontation and an excuse to wriggle out of their relationship. She had asked to break their engagement. He had hurt tremendously at that time and mourned for a while. Sharifah, however, found new love soon after, forgetting Shukri almost immediately. That was another blow to his broken heart. But that became a distant memory when he met Laura. He simply fell in love.

Firdaus had laughed at him then, calling him soft-hearted and a romantic. Shukri laughed with him, admiring the young man for his boisterousness. He knew that Firdaus was not as wayward as he pretended to be. Although Firdaus was flirtatious, he never went too far, always showing decorum and respect to the opposite sex when it fitted the situation. This was an attitude instilled by his upbringing as a good Malay lad from Johor.

"Just be careful, Shuk. You don't want to be disappointed again," Firdaus had said, breaking into Shukri's reverie.

Shukri smiled as he remembered the time he met Laura. It was at a drama presentation at the university auditorium. They were lined up to enter the establishment when she, who was standing in front of him, stepped back and trod on his foot. The heel that stabbed his Nike shoes right at his toe gave him a very painful sensation that made him grit his teeth.

"Oh, I am so sorry! Are you hurt?" the person in front of him exclaimed, turning around and holding his arm.

"It's all right. Don't worry," he answered, looking down into the most beautiful face he had ever seen.

She had smiled up at him tremulously, her hands on his arm, and he had smiled down at her reassuringly.

From then on, the two of them had been inseparable. They talked whenever they could. They would tell each other stories and talk about subjects that most others would not understand. About love and sacrifice. How love made people blind and make a drastic decision. It seemed to Shukri that he and Laura were made for each other in every respect.

One of the most interesting stories that Laura told him was about the legend of the harvest festival. To him it was a very beautiful story of unconditional love. He was fascinated with the Kadazan Dusun people's regard for the legend.

"A long time ago, there was Kinorohingan and his consort, Suminundu. They had a beautiful daughter called Huminodun. They lived in a land of plenty, where the people dwelled in peace and harmony until a famine beset the land ..."

Shukri had watched Laura tell the story in her own expressive way, looking at her luscious lips and her faraway eyes.

"The land was scoured far and wide for seeds to plant for raising food, but the effort was in vain. It was then that Suminundu sacrificed her only daughter so the people might eat. Huminodun was sacrificed in the cultivation area. Her body became the varieties of edible plants for the people: flesh made into rice; head into coconut; bones into tapioca; toes into ginger; teeth into maize; knees into yams; and other parts of her body into other edible plants. To this day, we honour the spirits of the paddy through our harvest festival.

"The beauty pageant is to commemorate Huminodun's sacrifice for the people. She was the epitome of filial duty and womanhood. She was obedient to her parents, respectful of the community, and selfless," Laura added.

She spoke about her community's respect for rice, saying that each grain that fell or was thrown out would "cry", and so the Dusuns were taught from a young age never to waste rice or allow it to fall from the plate.

Shukri had nodded and smiled at her, filling his senses with her beauty and the peacefulness that seemed to exude from her being.

During one of their debates and her bouts of sullenness, he had softly said, "My beautiful Huminodun, don't ever leave me. It would kill me."

She looked aghast, replying, "No … no! I am not worthy to be called Huminodun. She's perfection personified."

He understood at that time that the legend did not exist merely to shore up a belief; instead, it was real and genuine to the people.

The couple were together for the next three years. To Shukri, those were their happiest years, when they studied together before in the university and worked out their problems in their respective subjects together. They had gone through days of happiness and euphoria, and at times doom and gloom when their studies got tough. But they were together, happy in each other's company.

There were times, though, when Laura was in doubt about her future with him. Shukri understood how she felt. She was helplessly in love with him, but going to the next level with their relationship would require her to make the ultimate sacrifice, namely to leave her culture and tradition behind and embrace a new life that was alien to her. Her only beacon in this new life was Shukri.

This was proven when Shukri asked her father formally for his daughter's hand in marriage. The incident had caused a rift among the family members. It pained Shukri to see Laura so hurt.

On his trip back to his hometown, Shukri took a break from reminiscing and made a stop before his destination to place a call to Laura. No one answered the telephone, so he knew Laura was still peeved with him for going back to Bandar Muar. He was worried that she might change her mind about marrying him, but ultimately he believed that their love would persevere.

I can't just love you and not marry you, Laura. But I want to do this right, he thought as he started to drive again towards his home, which was still a fair distance away. While he drove, he thought of her parents and how they had reacted to his proposal to marry their daughter. He was embarrassed and rueful that they had taken it the way they had, but he was glad he'd had the gumption to ask.

"Do you think our daughter is part of the livestock? You come in and pick which one you want? Well, think again! If you have any shred of decency, and any regard for our culture and tradition, you should come with your parents and propose formally," Laura's father had stated angrily.

"Where are your parents? You should have proper respect as a visitor to this village! You are educated, are you not? And yet you show extreme ignorance," Mamai Mikol had added.

Shukri had been mortified, but he was still determined. "I just want to marry your daughter. If need be, I will inform my mother and uncle to come to Sabah. I am so sorry. I didn't know about your traditions."

"According to our tradition, if you like someone's daughter, you must send your representative or family members to propose, not just walk in and ask," Laura's mother had added.

"I will do that," Shukri had answered.

"No need. We will not accept your proposal. We don't want people not of our belief and ethnicity as our in-laws!" Laura's father said harshly, shutting down the possibility for Shukri to make any more arguments.

These events and more were what Shukri related to his mother as soon as he had settled into his childhood home the previous time he had returned for a visit. His mother's lovely face had appeared sad for him, yet she felt that he should get out of the situation.

"Shukri, there are other women out there. Why choose one that brings you a lot of grief like this?" she had said gently, smoothing back his hair.

"It saddens me that they did that to you. We are a courteous people, my son, and we have our own custom. I am disappointed that they treated you that way," his beautiful mother added, rather peeved.

"I don't know, Mother. I just can't help loving her. I can't imagine a life without her," he had told her.

She sighed sadly. "Is she worth all the insults and grief, Shukri? You are a good son. I am sure you see the best in her. But are you sure this is what you want? There are many women out there, you know," his mother had insisted gently.

Shukri understood why his mother felt that way. Laura was far away in Sabah and there were many young beautiful women in Johor. His mother believed that choosing one of those women to love and marry would not be difficult for him. But he could not help loving Laura. And he couldn't imagine not consummating his love in marriage and having her with him in his future.

Shukri imagined that his mother still felt the way she had during his previous visit. He sighed and dialled Laura's number again, but it rang to the end without any answer.

He drove on towards Muar, his thoughts fleeing to Laura and her parents, the latter of whom had vigorously opposed his proposal. His heart ached as he imagined Laura possibly leaving him.

I love her so much, and I am pretty sure she feels the same way about me. There must be a way for us to be happy together. I am sure that after a while, her parents will come to terms with our marriage and accept us for what we are, he thought.

He thought about their differences where their respective religious beliefs were concerned. He did not think that it should be a problem. There were many intermarriages and converts. Happiness and contentment in a marriage was not wholly ruled by one's ethnic background and belief system. Instead, attitude and aptitude in dealing with married life was what made a couple happy.

Shukri grinned as he imagined how happy he and Laura would be together. He imagined the beautiful young woman sitting on a gorgeously decorated wedding dais and smiling coyly at him. He smiled again, his happiness blossoming in his heart like a garden of flowers. He laughed at how corny his vision seemed, but he didn't care. He was in love after all.

I am going back to Kota Kinabalu to marry Laura. I am going to be her devoted lover and partner forever. I am going to make her happy, he thought.

Chapter 8

Laura missed Shukri so much that her heart seemed to ache. Standing alone at the beach, looking away towards the blue sea and the islands, she thought of him and his unaffected laughter and smile. She thought of his deep eyes fringed by thick eyelashes.

It had been a week since he returned to the Peninsula, but it seemed like forever to her. She felt his absence every minute when he was not around.

Looking at couples holding hands while walking along the waterfront, she sighed again. She wished that she and Shukri were together on a boat travelling towards the islands, where the sunset's glorious splendour filled the evening sky. She remembered their previous visits together to the island, diving into the deepness of the sea, enjoying the warm water and the sights therein.

"I miss you," she whispered, her eyes brimming with tears.

Flashbacks intruded into her thoughts. She remembered again how they had met and how their relationship had blossomed since the day she stepped on his brand-new Nike shoes.

The three years they had spent together had been full of joy and happiness for Laura, although Shukri's attempt to secure permission from her parents to marry her was a disaster, to say the least.

"After the convocation, I will marry you, Laura," Shukri had said one day, which had made her ecstatic, as she could not wait to be with him in every way, seeing that she adored him. She was therefore surprised when he told her that he was going back to his hometown to relax and find some peace of mind.

"Why?" she had asked tersely. Walking barefoot and legs touching the wet sand along the beach.

"I am in a state of confusion. I have related our predicament to my mother, and she has asked me to come home," he shared, looking into her face.

"Are you breaking up with me?" she asked, her heart beating fast.

"No ... no! I didn't mean it like that. I just need some peace of mind to think," he answered. "Don't ever think of it like that, my love. I will never do that to you. I love you very much. I promise." He held her hands tightly, looking into her eyes in order to convince her.

Laura had quietly looked away. She was disappointed and annoyed with Shukri, as he had promised to take her to meet his mother. She had hoped so much for that to happen as a sign of their impending marriage.

Shukri had sensed her angst and tried to make her understand, but she was too angry to actually listen to and assimilate his words.

"Laura, please try to understand. I don't want to lose you. If I could, I would just take you away from your family and live somewhere with you forever, but I need to do this the right way," he said, kissing her forehead.

Laura had backed away and pulled her hands from Shukri's grasp, which shocked him.

"You are just saying that. If you really love and care for me, then you should find a way for us to face this problem together," she had cried, tears brimming in her eyes.

"I don't want your relationship with your parents to be sullied, Laura. It would be wrong of me to let that happen. I want us to be a big happy family, not pulled every which way," Shukri had said, trying to explain.

"If you leave, our dreams will die," Laura had answered. "This is because my parents rejected your proposal, right?

"I love you, Shukri. I never loved anyone as I do you. But you are leaving me alone at a time when I am facing this problem."

"I am not leaving you. I just need to be on my own for a while," he answered, smiling down at her. He held her hands, telling her repeatedly that he loved her and would never leave her.

Laura, however, remained apprehensive. The thought of losing Shukri was too much for her to bear. She blurted out, "When you return, you might have a change of heart. You won't feel like that anymore, and maybe ..."

"Don't say another word. I will be back before the end of the semester break," Shukri had said, interrupting her.

"All right, Shukri. I hope you have a safe journey back to your hometown and that you find the peace of mind you seek there," Laura had answered.

Recalling the conversation, Laura felt uneasy and unhappy. There was so much she had wanted to say that she'd left unsaid. And yet could it have made a difference? She didn't know. She missed Shukri terribly.

Her mobile telephone rang, which made her jump. She immediately took it out of her handbag and saw that the caller was Shukri. She debated on whether she should answer the phone. She recalled that she had called and texted Shukri about three days before but hadn't managed to get through. He had neither answered her calls nor replied to her text.

The phone stopped ringing. She felt a tinge of regret that she had not answered it.

She was still angry that Shukri hadn't allowed her to go with him to meet his mother. It had left her feeling unappreciated and unloved, although deep inside she knew Shukri cared for her.

Her phone rang again. She decided not to answer it after all. *If he can ignore me, I can ignore him,* she thought rather petulantly. She knew that it was rather juvenile, but she didn't feel particularly sensible at the moment.

In thinking about being sensible, her new housemate, Nonie, came to mind, Nonie was a pretty young woman from Sarawak. The girl was very sensible and advised Laura not to frequent the waterfront. To Nonie it was a bad place where untoward incidents could happen.

"Don't go there alone, Laura. You never know what can happen in such places. I heard about bad incidents happening there, especially to women who frequent that place alone – even our university mates," she had stated.

"I am all right, Nonie. I won't go to the back alley. There are many people there, tourists, diners … Thanks anyway. I will remember that."

As darkness fell and the neon lights of the city came on, Laura felt that it was time to go back home. Getting into her car, she drove slowly away from the busy city streets. Her phone rang again, but she ignored it.

She admired the neon lights of the city, and the harbour where ships awaited to unload their cargoes. *Such beauty in everyday sights,* she thought.

There were cars parked along the Likas Bay area, and several young people were dancing in the open space. *They must be foreigners,* Laura thought, *illegal immigrants.* They seemed to be everywhere.

Driving a little faster, she recalled a news item about a couple who were robbed of their valuables in that area.

"Try coming near my car and I will run you over," Laura muttered.

The social problems caused by these young illegal immigrants were countless. Many of them had been caught stealing, robbing, and even molesting other people, especially locals.

"Hmm. I wonder what these people's parents taught them. … Maybe they were never taught about decency and respect," Laura muttered.

She drove home safely, going through the night thinking about her parents and missing Shukri.

Chapter 9

After having lunch and Mamai Mikl went down to feed Kopi, his dog, Jenny and Inai Ulis sat on the floor facing the door looking at Mamai Mikol feeding Kopi.

"Poor Laura. I didn't even manage to talk to her, Jenny," Inai Ulis said, looking at her daughter. She was a little sad that she had not been able to speak when Laura called. It was not that she hadn't wanted to. She had just been lost for words.

"It's better that you call her, Mother," Jenny answered, smiling.

"Why don't you dial her number then, Jenny? I want to talk to her," the elderly woman said.

Jenny was fast with her fingers. Soon, her sister was answering the phone on the other end.

"Hi, Sis. It's Mother! She wants to talk to you," Jenny spoke into the phone.

"Mother … can you hear me?" Laura's voice through the phone sounded tinny and far away.

"Laura … yes, I can hear you. How are you? How is your baby?" Inai Ulis answered.

"We are both fine, Mother. My baby was quite big at birth, three kilos, so they had to do a caesarean section on me," Laura answered, excited to tell her mother about her baby.

Inai Ulis was sad to hear that her daughter had had to go through such a painful procedure when giving birth, but she was also happy that mother and child were healthy. She missed her daughter very much. The young woman's voice was enough to make her tear up.

"Are you following through with the rules of confinement, Laura?" the concerned mother asked.

"Rules of confinement? What is that?" Laura asked, mystified. She had never heard such a phrase before.

Inai Ulis was apprehensive, worried that her daughter might not have avoided the tribal taboo after giving birth. It was even more imperative that Laura follow the rules of confinement since she had undergone a C-section.

"You must follow the rules of confinement for forty-four days, Laura. Listen, you must not bathe in cold water during that period. Also, you must not eat fish with sharp fins. You must cover your feet and not stub your toe on anything," Inai Ulis shared. "Don't leave your child alone in the room. If you do, place a mirror near her face. You must adhere to all these practices, Laura, if you want to be healthy until your old age," she added.

"If you were here, I would be able to give you herbs and our traditional medicine to ensure your health," she said, pressing her point.

"Please don't worry, Mother. I am fine here. Shukri bought a lot of vitamins and many traditional medicines," Laura answered reassuringly.

"Take care of yourself, Laura. Be careful with what you eat and drink, and get a lot of rest so that you will be strong and get better faster. You must be stringent in your confinement," Inai Ulis said.

"I will, Mother. I love you, Mother. Send my regards to Father," Laura said, ending the conversation.

Inai Ulis sat there, the mobile phone forgotten in her hands. Her eyes shimmered with tears as she thought about Laura so far away with a newborn baby, taken care of by her mother-in-law.

She was not happy with the situation, as she felt that it was her duty to take care of her daughter during her confinement. She wanted to take care of her child just like her mother had taken care of her when she gave birth more than twenty-eight years ago to her first baby. Her people had very strict rules regarding the confinement. New mothers were usually bathed with herbs and normally drank traditional medicine acquired from the jungle.

Inai Ulis's mother was well versed in traditional medicine. She had garnered the knowledge from her mother, Inai Ulis's grandmother. With this knowledge, she had scoured the jungle at the foot of Mount Kinabalu to pick herbs and to gather chips of bark from certain trees to brew as medicine. She had a knowledge of herbs as well as some experience with the rites and liturgies of priestesses. With such wisdom, she was chosen as the village head later in her life.

During her own confinement, Inai Ulis endured all the attention from her mother, drinking the bitter herbal brews, bathing in fragrant warm water, and not having any visitors.

Thinking of Laura, she wondered if her daughter was really adhering to the confinement rules. She believed that whatever her daughter's postnatal treatment was, it was not as rigorous or proper as hers. To her, modern medicines of any form were all made from chemicals and were far inferior to her traditional medicines.

Chapter 10

Jenny watched her mother as the elderly woman looked out into the distance. She was happy that her mother had agreed to speak to her elder sister. She had been in constant contact with Laura but had never told her parents of this, as she hadn't wanted them to be angry at her. It was as if her parents had wanted to erase Laura's name from their minds. Any reminder of their firstborn evoked a negative response from them.

"Mother, why are you sad? You should be happy that Laura and the baby are well," Jenny said, rubbing her mother's back.

"Oh, I am happy. I was happy to speak to Laura," Inai Ulis said. "I just feel that I should be there for her at this time. All mothers should be with their daughters when they give birth."

"It's okay, Mother. She will come home after her confinement. I believe she wants you and Father to see her baby," Jenny said, comforting her mother.

Inai Ulis felt a stab of apprehension upon hearing this information. She was very happy to hear that Laura was coming home, as she would be able to see her first grandchild, but she was worried about how Mamai Mikol would react. She was not looking forward to his ranting about Laura again.

Inai Ulis had forgiven Laura a long time ago, but she was not too sure about her husband.

"Mother, you don't look too happy about Laura coming home. Why?" Jenny inquired, watching her mother's face, which showed several expressions in succession.

"I am very happy to hear that Laura wants to come home, but I am apprehensive about your father's reaction. What if he cannot forgive her?"

"You can persuade him to do so, Mother," Jenny answered.

Inai Ulis almost laughed. Getting her husband to change his mind was a monumental task, especially where forgiving Laura was concerned. He was set on holding on to his anger. After evicting his daughter from the house two years ago, his rants about her had not let up, especially when her name was mentioned.

"Your father's attitude is beyond me, Jenny," Inai Ulis said tersely.

"I will tell Father then. If he gets angry, there is nothing I can do about it. I just want to convey the message," Jenny answered. She believed that it was time for forgiveness and that her sister should return to the fold and be loved like before. She also believed that her mother had forgiven Laura and was just waiting to see her grandchild. The intuition and conscience of a mother was always to love her child, no matter what sins the child had committed against her. Inai Ulis was no exception to this rule.

Inai Ulis was no longer young. Her face was lined, and her once smouldering eyes were dull. She deserved to be happy, that's what Jenny says in her heart.

How Mother must be suffering on account of all the discontentment and trouble in the family. Even watching her and Father is painful. How much more must they be suffering from this problem now that Laura has had a child, Jenny thought. She recalled happier days when she was a younger child. In those days, she and her sister admired their father's musical talent and would spend hours listening to his rendition of old traditional songs. Together they would listen to him talk about the moon and the stars. One of his tales was about a line of stars that seemed to point towards the moon on certain clear nights. He told them that it meant a commoner was marrying a prince.

To this, Jenny had once replied that one day when the stars were aligned accordingly, a handsome prince would come to marry her. This had been followed by laughter from everybody who had been listening.

"Wishful thinking, Jenny. There is no king here." Laura had laughed at Jenny. Their father had chuckled with her.

"You never know. Grandmother once told us about the Chinese prince who fell in love with a local maiden here and married her," Jenny answered.

"Well, her prince left her and she died of a broken heart," their father had stated, sipping his coffee and looking at his two beloved daughters.

Their mother's entrance from the kitchen broke their discussion. She was carrying a tray of rice wrapped in banana leaves. The fragrance of the new rice permeated the air. The girls and their father each eagerly took a portion off the tray.

"Mmm, my all-time favourite, rice in banana leaves. I especially like those that are cooked with yam," Mamai Mikol said, smiling at Inai Ulis.

"I will go to my yam patch tomorrow and see if there are any old enough to dig," Inai Ulis said to her husband, taking her own portion of wrapped rice and eating it with the accompanying vegetables.

Jenny looked away into the night, thinking of those simpler, more innocent times when her family was happy. She missed those days of simplicity. Each evening, her father would play the seruling or the *sompoton* as Laura and Jenny did their homework or indulged in idle chatter.

If my sister was here, we would be a family again, looking at the stars and moon, telling stories, and eating wrapped rice, Jenny thought.

Since her sister had gotten married and moved to Kuala Lumpur to live, Jenny and her parents seldom sat at the veranda looking out upon the beauty of nature. They seldom told stories or even talked. There was something missing in their life. They tried to fill the void through their respective work. Once in a while, Jenny's father would sit at the veranda to drink his coffee, but he remained unsmiling at those times.

Chapter 11

"You raised me up so I could stand on the mountain. I am strong when I am on your shoulders. When you raise me up, the more I can be …"

Laura was seated at her leather sofa in her house, listened to the song and thought about her parents, especially her mother. She was happy to have spoken to her mother, but she had not always felt happy when her thoughts drifted to Inai Ulis.

Laura remembered when she was pregnant. Every day she had cried because she missed her mother. She had thought of her mother's love and about all her mother's sacrifices. She wished that she had not hurt her parents' feelings like she had.

At the time, she was soon to be a mother herself. Perhaps it was just her emotions that had gotten the better of her, but listening to that song when she was pregnant had made her sad and teary. She wanted to cry her heart out, as if the song was tormenting her instead of soothing her mind. She remembered how she hurts both of her parents by refusing to follow her parents advice, not to marry Shukri, a Muslim man who came from Johor, Penusilar Malaysia, Malaya as known by her parents. She felt how ungrateful child she is but her love to Shukri is too strong.

"Mother, forgive me," she had whispered, as the baby kicked in her stomach. She thought of herself as a baby in her mother's womb, carried with so much care and love even as her mother eked out a living off the land. How much more tiring and exhausting it must have been for Inai Ulis to be pregnant than it was for Laura.

Motherhood, Laura found out, was not that simple. She began to empathise with her mother, especially given the latter's position. She now understood that her mother wanted the best for her in life, in her own way. Laura had been hard-headed and rebellious, a terrible way for a child to be with her parents.

When she was with child, Laura missed home very much – the fresh mountain air, the sounds of birds in the morning, and the greenery around her childhood home. She missed the sounds of her parents' voices as they chatted in the morning before going off to do their respective work.

She had caressed her stomach, thinking about her baby and how she would have told her mother about her pregnancy if only her parents had approved of and blessed her marriage.

"I wish I could fly away home and hug my mother," she had said to herself. Her tears spilled when she remembered the last time she had seen Inai Ulis.

"How can you do this to us?!" her mother had cried.

"We don't want you to marry that man from Malaya!" her father had shouted.

At that time, Laura had persisted, stressing that she loved Shukri and saying that nothing would change her mind about marrying him.

"Why do you hate people from the Peninsula?" Laura had asked, getting very irritated with her parents' hard-headedness.

"You are a village girl, Laura. You are not worthy," her mother had quipped, much to Laura's chagrin.

"You have never heard of how they treat our women, Laura? How women from the island are lied to and humiliated, and how their passports are withheld so they can't come home?" her father had ranted.

She had recalled a story her aunt once told about a young woman from the village who had married a soldier from the Peninsula. The woman had gone back to her husband's hometown and was mistreated badly by his family.

"They are not all like that, Father. And nowadays the situation is not the same as before. If it happens with me with Shukri, I am not that stupid. I can always come home. We don't need a passport anymore. We use our identity cards," Laura had argued.

"That's not the main problem, Laura. We don't want you to convert to Islam," her mother had stressed, slowly but firmly.

Laura had stared at her mother in consternation.

"But Mother, all religions are the same. They stress a belief in God and in doing good to others. No religion promotes hate or enmity," Laura had argued.

"All right then! It's up to you. Go get married to that man! Get out of my house!" her father had shouted at her, pointing at the door.

"Never come back here ever again! In fact, don't call us your parents! Just get out!" the elderly man had yelled. His heart beats fast as if he is going to die. His tears rolled down as he pushed his daughter away from the house.

"Mother … please. I love our family, but I also love Shukri so much. I have decided to marry him. Forgive me," Laura had pleaded.

Her mother had stared at her stone-faced, the hurt, anger, and sadness expressed in turns on her face. Inai Ulis had stood up and left her daughter sitting there. Subsequent visits had resulted in the same thing. Her parents never backed down in their decision to disapprove of her marriage.

Her wedding had been a happy affair, but there had been a tinge of sadness.

Prior to the ceremony, Laura's aunt Sarah had said, "In two weeks, you will be wedded." Laura had realised that soon she would be married to Shukri.

"The wedding seems meaningless, Aunt. Especially without my parents' blessings. They are not even attending," Laura had answered.

"I went through a similar experience when I married my husband. In fact, my family actually beat me after throwing me out of the house. I still have a scar to show for it," Sarah answered, lifting her skirt and showing Laura the long scar on her leg.

Laura had stared at the scar, which started from just above the heel and went right up to the back of her aunt's knee. She felt rather frightened. Her father had never hit her to cause a scar like that.

"I was brought up by my grandmother after my parents died in an accident. She loved me very much, but her brother beat me up when she told him that I wanted to marry a Muslim. He actually tried to stab me with a knife, but I managed to move away. He could only cut my leg," Sarah shared. "I don't know why the people of this village get angry when they hear about women wanting to marry men from the Peninsula," she added.

"Maybe in the past when soldiers from the Peninsula were sent here, they didn't respect our culture and traditions," Laura answered.

"I don't know, Laura, but maybe the men in the village just disliked those men and created these unsavoury rumours to discredit them," Sarah offered. "They tell their parents these tales, and of course the elderly believe them. The hate and animosity is then perpetuated," she added thoughtfully.

Laura nodded in agreement, feeling woeful. She didn't know how long her parents would hold their anger against her.

During her wedding, Laura had sat demurely on the dais, but her eyes searched the crowd for her parents' faces. Her smile was tremulous, as she did not see them, but she held her posture, trying to make it through the ceremony.

"The most important thing is that you are now Shukri's wife," her uncle Ustad Naim had said. Laura had nodded. She looked at the man whom her aunt Sarah had risked her family's displeasure to marry.

Standing in her room one day, Laura had almost staggered as her flashbacks made her very tired and weary. She shored up her inner strength with the thought that she would be a mother soon. She believed that the baby would be, in a way, a knot that would tie the marriage more tightly and deepen the love she and Shukri had for each other.

Chapter 12

The rain was heavy that evening, beating hard on the pavement outside with a low roar. Laura looked out of her window and watched the rain as it began to fill the drains. They eventually overflowed, spilling the water onto the road. To Laura, it looked like an impending flood.

Her husband wasn't home yet. She imagined that he had gotten stuck in a traffic jam on his way home from work. Noting that traffic jams seemed to occur more frequently on rainy days, she hoped that Shukri would reach home soon, safe and sound.

She sighed and turned away, walking to her room to peep in on the baby, who was sleeping soundly. The baby at one month old looked so peaceful and angelic in slumber. Laura looked around at the sparse furnishings and thought about her mother-in-law's home, which was neatly decorated and fully furnished. She had stayed with her mother-in-law for a month, but she'd left after becoming uneasy around her sister-in-law's cute but boisterous children.

"You are still in confinement, Laura. Do stay longer," Shukri's mother had told her, but she had insisted on going back to their own apartment after a month. She wanted some peace and quiet, away from the children.

"I will be all right, Mother. I promise to take it easy and to get a lot of rest," Laura had said. She was quite relieved when the older woman gave in. The drive back, from Johor to Kuala Lumpur, was enjoyable. Settling into their apartment of six months was even more delightful.

She, of course, had all day to herself in the apartment, as Shukri went to work each day and would only return late in the evening. The famous traffic jams always held him up. As usual when alone, Laura thought of home and wished she could just go back to her village and relax. She thought of the various quaint walkways that meandered through the shrubs and led to her parents' home, with the bamboo walls and floor, and the palm frond roof. She also envisioned the green paddy plants that swayed gently when the wind blew. The cold spring water where she took her bath was something she also missed. She thought of the lengths of bamboo fashioned together to bring water closer to home, before the wonders of pipes brought water into homes. Their water was not treated but was from a pure spring in the mountains. As for lights, the village had only been wired for electricity the day Laura was born.

Thinking of the easy camaraderie in her village, she wondered about city dwellers, who always kept to themselves. Neighbours hardly knew one another. They did not even greet one another. Laura found this a little upsetting. It made her miss home even more.

She thought of the harmonious existence in her village, where the people came together to help their neighbours in community work. Everyone knew everybody else, and the people always gathered together for celebrations and festivals. She missed the closeness among the people in her community.

Thinking about the villagers made her miss her parents too. She missed being with them and listening to their chats. She admired their tenacity in tending the land, which was not an easy job. Planting rice, yams, and tapioca, as well as vegetables, for their sustenance and for the market was their daily chore, and they never seemed to let up. The money that they earned for their hard work had gone towards buying household essentials and paying for their children's education.

Laura felt guilty about having been disobedient to her parents and hurting them in the process. She cried as she thought of them.

Her baby awoke and started to cry, startling her out of her reverie. She went into her room and, taking up her baby, began to hum. The tune was one her grandmother Odu Madilin had sung to her and Jenny when they were children, but she couldn't remember the lyrics.

She cried a little as she hummed the song, but she stopped when she remembered her mother's advise to her not to cry too much during her confinement. She was told that it could make her sick.

She recalled a story about an aunt who had gotten sick during her confinement period and had remained in a very bad shape until Laura's grandmother Odu Madilin treated the aunt with traditional herbs found in the jungle. It was not an easy period for her aunt.

It was believed that one could die if one did not adhere to the traditional norms during the confinement period. Some women were known to have been paralyzed or to have gone mad after getting sick during the confinement period.

"Be careful with what you eat and drink during the confinement period," Laura's mother had told her through the phone, her voice gentle and solicitous.

Remembering her mother's voice made Laura cry again. She wished she could just pack up and go home. She wanted to be her parents' child again, just be at home and be part of the family again.

As she thought of the tranquillity of nature in the village, her father's harsh words uttered in parting thundered again into her memory, making her flinch.

"Get out! Never come back." She remembered the words, the shout of rage from her father. She remembered stumbling away from her family's haven. As she walked away, she was crying so hard that could not see properly, which caused her to fall over obstacles and into potholes.

Laura gazed at her sleeping child and felt the love swell in her heart. Natasha, her baby girl, was beautiful with light brown hair like her paternal grandmother's, and fair skin like Laura's mother's.

"My mother will love Natasha. She will fall in love with this beautiful baby," Laura said, smiling down at the sleeping cherub. She remembered that her mother had wanted many children but had had only two girls.

The doorknob being turned marked Shukri's return. Laura looked up to smile at her husband, who immediately entered the bedroom to stroke his baby's hair.

"Don't touch the baby as soon as you come in, dear," Laura said, still smiling up at her husband as she gently brushed his hands away from the child. She took his laptop case from him and set it aside.

"Not done with the taboo?" asked Shukri, leaning forward to kiss her forehead.

"It's in my blood, dear. Tradition must be followed. I don't want anything bad to happen," said Laura. "My grandmother said that it's not good if you go to see your newborn baby directly upon reaching home. It is believed that an evil entity can get to the child easily," said Laura.

Shukri shrugged. "Yes, you are right, dear. We'll follow what's appropriate, not superstition," Shukri answered, hugging her. Laura laid her head on her beloved husband's shoulder.

"Laura, your eyes are red. Did you cry again?" her husband whispered affectionately. Laura shook her head. Shukri stared into her eyes and sighed. Knowing that she had been crying, he felt sorry for her. "You have to learn to stay calm. Don't think too much. Since we got married, you've been like this. I don't want you to continue being sad.

"I am worried you might get sick," Shukri said, watching his wife's face. "Sometimes I feel as if you regretted your decision to marry me," he said, still studying her face. His right hand lifted her chin so he could gently kiss her lips. "Do you regret it, Laura?" he asked, continuing to gaze at his wife's face.

"I don't want people to talk about how skinny you are when we go back to Kota Kinabalu. I don't want anybody to think I didn't take good care of you. No regrets, I hope."

"No, dear, there's nothing to regret," answered Laura.

"Laura, if there's any problem, don't keep it inside. And don't cry," said Shukri. "Say anything. We will talk it out together," he said, standing up and walking towards the table. He reached for the cold drink that had been placed there earlier. Then he sat back down next to his wife.

"Dear?" Laura sighed deeply.

"Yes, dear?" said Shukri, raising his eyebrows.

"I want to go back home," she said slowly. Shukri looked surprised and stopped sipping the drink.

"You want to go home? Why?" asked Shukri in consternation.

"I miss Mother and Father and Jenny, and I miss my hometown," she answered. Her tears began to spill.

"Laura, please, do not cry," urged Shukri. "I will not stop you if you really want to go home. But wait until you've recovered. Then we can both go home."

"You want to come back home with me?" she asked as she gazed at her husband.

"Why? Can't I?"

"You're not afraid of being chased away again?" Laura asked, her eyes shimmering with tears. She was both amazed and surprised that her husband would consider going back with her after all the trouble they had been through.

"This time it will be both of us. I do not believe your father will have the heart to shun Natasha. Grandparents would never chase away a newborn baby like her. Moreover, both her grandparents are people of good character," Shukri said gently.

"You do not hate my parents?" Laura asked.

"Hate? Where did you learn this?" said Shukri, tickling her nose. "Do you know what hate is? I respect and love my father-in-law and mother-in-law, you know?" he said, smiling.

"If they had not given birth to and educated the woman I love most in this world, surely I would be the most miserable person on earth. But they gave me their daughter, who made me the happiest person alive.

"Why should I hate them?" Shukri asked, kissing his wife.

Laura smiled, exulting in the fact that she would be home soon. She stared ahead, remembering beautiful nights with stars and moonlight.

Memories engulfed her. She remembered her family enjoying the beauty and uniqueness of God's creation, the green virgin forest away from the pollution of air and culture.

I hope there will be forgiveness in your heart, Father and Mother, she thought as she hugged her baby close to her chest. Shukri was now sitting in front of his laptop in the study, busy with work he had brought home. Laura sighed. She closed the bedroom door quietly and lay on the bed. Her thoughts went back to the blessed land of Sabah where she was born and raised, and educated to be a person of high morals.

*   *   *

Shukri awoke to the sound of Natasha crying. He checked the baby's diaper and changed it before patting her back gently. Seeming to know that her father was tired, Natasha fell asleep instantly with a smile on her face. Shukri covered her with a blanket.

Shukri looked at Laura, who was still asleep and hadn't heard the baby cry. *She must be tired from crying,* he thought. He stared at the face of a woman he loved so dearly, the woman who had been willing to sacrifice everything – her religion and even her family – to be with him. As he lay down beside his beloved wife, his mind wandered to the day five years ago when their seeds of love began to grow.

"I'm afraid to accept your love," Laura had said when Shukri continued to send love texts to her. It had been difficult for him to capture the heart of a girl who adamantly adhered to the customs of her tribe. It took months of pleading for him to convince her that he truly loved her. Shukri smiled and thought how grateful he was to have found Laura, as compared to his ex-fiancée, Sharifah, a shy and well-mannered young woman who, however, was too demanding and self-centred.

He vowed not to let his wife's sacrifice be in vain. Her request to go home to her family would be fulfilled. He wanted to prove that he was a responsible man unlike the Malayan men Laura's people had heard about before.

Shukri remembered how he had ventured to seek Laura's hand in marriage, going alone to her village as a mature man capable of making his own decisions.

"Where are your parents?" Laura's father had asked. "This isn't like the western country where you can take anyone you like and then just throw them away when you don't need them anymore!" Laura's father had snapped at him.

"My apologies. My father died long ago. I have only my mother," Shukri had said in a trembling voice.

"Do you think marriage is a game?" Mikol continued. "We have traditions to uphold! It is not a game!" The vision of Laura's father telling him off and mentioning how he disliked Malayan men still played in his mind.

"You have no job and are still studying, yet you dare to speak of your desire to marry my daughter." Shukri had felt like a prisoner waiting for the gallows, quietly listening to the tirades of the older man.

"What are you going to feed my daughter? Rocks?"

His question startled Shukri, who felt embarrassed. Mamai Mikol was right, as Shukri did not have a job at the time. His aim had been to make Laura his wife before other men could capture her heart. He was sure that Laura's father wouldn't understand his feeling.

"Get a job! Prove that you can take care of my daughter! Do you think love is enough?!"

Shukri had been challenged by Laura's father, but he remained calm since he was at her parents' home. He could've just abandoned his plan to marry Laura and let fate decide their future, but he didn't want to lose her.

With patience and willpower, the couple were finally wed, albeit without Laura's parents' approval. Shukri hoped that with Natasha's birth, Inai Ulis and Mamai Mikol would change their minds and allow the young couple to return home as family.

Shukri looked at Laura's face and kissed her forehead lightly. Both Laura and Natasha smiled in their sleep as if they were dreaming the same dream. *Maybe they are dreaming about Mount Kinabalu,* he thought, smiling.

He remembered a conversation long ago about the mountain.

"Since you lived at the foot of the mountain, you must have climbed it many times, right?" he had asked Laura when he first found out where her hometown was.

"No, never," she replied, blushing.

"People pay a lot of money to climb that mountain, but you have never been up there?" asked Shukri.

"The mountain is a sacred place for us," she said. Then she added, "Before our people may climb it, offerings must be given in the form of food, especially white chicken."

"Why?"

"Because for our people, the peak is our final resting place."

Shukri never again asked raised the sensitive issue.

"It's their belief. We should have respect for them," he'd told his friends and lecturers during their trip to climb the mountain. Laura did not join them.

Chapter 13

"Mikol, Mother is very sick," Inai Ulis said to her husband as he arrived from the nearby village.

"Are you from Mother's house?" she asked the woman who accompanied him, looking at her faded headcloth.

"She's very ill." The woman sighed. Mamai Mikol often took vitamins and nutritious beverages for his mother, but she always refused to take them. She preferred to have the traditional drink she made out of roots and herbs.

"You have to take the vitamins, Mother. It will help you to get well," Inai Ulis had told her before. Odu Madilin had never been keen on modern medicines. She did not believe they could cure her illness.

"I don't need the medicine, Ulis. I'm old. Just let me die in peace."

She was growing senile in her old age. Sometimes she would call out to her children and grandchildren, and when they all gathered at her house, she would scold them.

Her children knew she had dementia. She was ninety years old but was still capable of climbing uphill and doing farm work – until she slipped and fell downhill a few months back.

Inai Ulis was sad. Her mother-in-law never seemed to know the meaning of rest. She would be all over the hill planting paddy, or scouring the woods to find herbs and wild vegetables to sell at the market or for her own use. Neighbours and friends advised her to rest, but she replied by saying the more she stayed at home, the weaker she got.

"Did she take any medication?" Inai Ulis asked Mamai Mikol.

"You know her. She wouldn't take modern medicine. She prefers sap from medicinal plants, which is hard to find during the rainy season." Some saps could be toxic if they weren't prepared properly.

Odu Madilin had taught her children about traditional medicines and how to find them in the woods near their house. It was an important aspect of their lives, the knowledge of deriving medicines from plants.

Both Mamai Mikol and Inai Ulis startled when they heard Jona calling them in haste. Gasping for breath, Jona who is Mamai Mikol youngest sister, grabbed Mamai Mikol's hand and pulled him with her, waving her other hand at Inai Ulis. "Mother is very sick! Hurry!" They ran together to their mother's house.

"I hope she's all right." Inai Ulis's mind raced with her steps. "She was fine when I left her earlier."

They arrived ten minutes later. The family had already gathered at the house. Pale and weak, Odu Madilin spoke to her children and grandchildren and tried hard to give them final hugs.

Upon her last breath, there were cries of sadness from the women and girls surrounding her. Inai Ulis was speechless. She couldn't believe that her mother was no longer with them. The old woman's face was calm, as if she was sleeping in peace.

"She's no longer in pain," said one of her grandchildren, crying. The atmosphere was rife with the sounds of crying. Inai Ulis and Mamai Mikol stood over the strong old lady and covered her body with a piece of batik cloth.

"I have no one to turn to anymore," cried Inai Ulis. Her mother-in-law had always scolded her and annoyed Inai Ulis, but Odu Madilin and her husband had showered their daughter-in-law with moral support when her husband left her.

She remembered Odu Madilin sending a sack of rice to her house when she was out working for extra money. Odu Madilin didn't like the fact that her daughter-in-law worked, as she was embarrassed by the villagers' gossip about her irresponsible son who had left Inai Ulis for another woman. Inai Ulis had had to work at the time to earn money for her children's school fees and books.

Odu Madilin had been a mother to Inai Ulis in every way after she was married to Mikol, which happened when she was very young. Ulis's real mother had passed away, and her father had married a widow from the nearby village. The relationship between Ulis and her father was never close. Now, the death of her mother-in-law triggered Inai Ulis's memories of how hard her life had been after Mamai Mikol left. Remembering her daughter Laura, whom she had chased out of the house, she wailed in sorrow.

"I am going to town to ask Ailin's son, Samin, to broadcast the news," Mamai Mikol told his wife. The sound of gongs echoed in the village to mark a death. Mamai Mikol knew only Samin can assist to drive to Radio Sabah to do the announcement immediately. Samin is the only son of Ailin who married to his older brother that had passed away 10 years ago.

Soon neighbours and people from nearby villages came to pay their respects and offer their condolences while offering whatever assistance they could give.

Inai Ulis lamented further when she remembered that Laura had been very close to Odu Madilin.

*   *   *

That night, the house was ablaze with lights. Relatives came to pay their last respects, sitting around the body sombrely. They wept for the deceased. Some spoke about Odu Madilin's good character, while others lamented that she should have rested and no longer gone up into the hills to cultivate the land.

The dirges of the grieving masses were tremendous, indicating that Odu Madilin had been a well-respected and well-loved member of the community.

Mamai Mikol stayed calm, although he was very sad that his mother was no longer with him. After all, he was handling the funeral and was expected to remain composed.

"Have all our relatives been informed?" asked an old man who sat outside among the group at the compound.

"Yes, we had it broadcast this morning," Mikol answered. "Mother told us before that when she died, she wanted to be buried next to Father."

"Yes, that's good. Hopefully there is still space there. Otherwise, we could place her at the nearest spot," the old man said. Mamai Mikol nodded his head. As Mamai Mikol didn't have much else to say, he went back into the house.

Still sitting near the body of Odu Madilin, Inai Ulis watched Mamai Mikol from a distance.

I grieve over the loss of my mother-in-law, who was a mother to me. She helped me a lot. Mikol must be grieving hard too, she thought, feeling sorry for her husband, who looked lost among the grieving crowd.

Outside the house, she could see more people arrive to pay their last respects. In three days, the well-respected former village chief who was wise but straightforward in imparting wisdom would be buried and they would no longer see her.

Chapter 14

"Sis, there is bad news from the village." Laura's heart skipped a bit as she listened to the trembling voice of Jenny on the phone. "Grandmother has passed away!"

"Dear God! What happened to her? Was she sick? Why didn't you let me know earlier?" Laura knew very well that Odu Madilin, a strict woman, had never been stingy about imparting knowledge. She had taught Laura a great deal about wild herbs and traditional medicine. "How is Father taking this?"

"I feel sorry for him, as he seems in shock. Otherwise he is all right."

"How many days has it been?"

"Just an hour ago," said Jenny.

Laura took a deep breath. "I'll come home as soon as possible, Jenny."

"Will Shukri allow you?"

"Yes."

"That's great! I am glad you can come back! I'll let Mother and Father know."

Jenny hung up. Laura took another deep breath and thought about how to proceed. She wanted to go home to pay her last respects to her late grandmother. It seemed the right time for her to go back and see her family.

My parents will never chase Natasha out, she thought as she recalled her colleagues talking about the terrible fate they had endured when they got married to someone not favoured by their parents. But after a while, their parents had a change of heart after seeing their new grandchildren, subsequently accepting their sons and daughters back into their family.

One of Laura's friends who had undergone this type of ordeal was Rosilah. She had been banished from her own family when she got married to a man who her mother had remarked had the face of a drug addict. After Rosilah had her baby, her family accepted her back into their life. Laura was happy to hear these stories of sorrow and subsequent joy that were similar to hers.

"Apparently I'm not alone. There are friends who are in the same boat as me," she whispered. Laura believed that parents loved their children to the end, no matter how the children had fallen out of favour.

Laura called Shukri to let him know of her grandmother's passing and to ask for his permission to return to her village.

"All right, Laura, we will go together. I'll buy the plane tickets. You pack what we need."

She smiled, thinking that she loved him for his patience and perseverance in dealing with her.

As she packed, her thoughts went to her parents. *Will they accept us? Will they ask us to go away? Will they accept Natasha?*

Later that day, Shukri arrived home and told her that they were going to fly to Kota Kinabalu that evening. Laura was touched by his kindness and understanding at a time such as this one.

"Our flight is at three o'clock. We'll have lunch at the airport. What happened to Grandmother?" he asked.

"She fell down a hill. After that, her condition worsened. She couldn't walk. Jenny said it was sudden."

"Life and death is in the hands of God, Laura. We have to accept the will of the Divine," said Shukri, tying his shoelaces. He checked around the living room and bedroom, turning off all lights and locking all doors.

They left the house with Laura holding Natasha tight.

"Hopefully all will go well, dear," said Shukri when they were in the elevator. Laura sighed. She understood what he meant. "You have to be strong."

Shukri's friend Suhaimi was waiting for them at the car. "My condolences to you and your family, madam," said Suhaimi.

"Thank you," replied Laura.

Shukri told Suhaimi about the trip and their plans. Suhaimi understood their situation and shared his friend's concern. This would be the couple's first time in Laura's home village after having been banished.

"Everything will be fine, dear," whispered Shukri to Laura.

Laura smiled at him, but her mind continued to drift between sorrow for the loss of her grandmother to missing her parents and fearing what their reaction to her would be. She and Shukri hadn't told her parents that they were coming home.

Jenny has probably told them by now, Laura thought. "What will they say to me?" she wondered aloud quietly.

"We're going home, Huminodun," Shukri said, smiling at her. Laura stared into her husband's face without smiling back, as her mind had started to drift away again.

"Is this God's will to give us a chance to make peace within the family?" she wondered, recalling the time after her grandfather had passed away and how Odu Madilin had cried for the man she loved. She was now united with her husband in the final resting place in the netherworld, accessed through a portal in Mount Kinabalu.

Laura could imagine the villagers and relatives getting busy for the funeral. She was almost able to see the faces of the bereaved.

"Dear … I'm worried," she murmured softly, glancing at her husband.

"Do not worry, dear. God is always with us, remember?"

"Hmm, but I'm still worried, scared, and sad," she murmured as she gazed at her husband.

"Have faith in God," whispered Shukri. He held her hands, Laura gripped his hand tightly and they seated at the back seat of the car.

Laura longed for her family. This was her first time visiting her childhood home as a married woman, even though the actual cause was to pay her respects to her grandmother before the latter was buried. Laura continued to praise God, asking that he grant her and her young family acceptance back into her parents' family.

The flight to Kota Kinabalu was uneventful. As the silver bird took them over the South China Sea towards the island of Borneo, Laura's thoughts were already home.

Laura performed the formality of unbuckling her seat belt after landing almost automatically; the same was true as she and Shukri claimed their luggage and walked out of the airport. Once again the couple stood on Sabah ground, but this time they had an addition, their baby, Natasha.

Chapter 15

The sound of the funeral gong echoed through the village. Laura and Shukri, with their baby, travelled in a taxi towards her parents' house. Laura knew that the gong was to announce the passing of a resident. Shukri looked at Laura's sorrowful face and held her hands tightly. He was experiencing inner turbulence, as he would be facing his in-laws again.

The car stopped at Laura's parents' house. The couple disembarked and began to take out their luggage. The house looked deserted.

"Mother, Father!" Laura called. She walked around the perimeter of the house to look for them. Then she went into the house and looked into the rooms, calling them. It was then that she realised they were probably at her grandmother's house.

"Stay here and rest, dear, I will go and look for them after I rest a little," Shukri said. He looked around the familiar living room. The photographs were still mounted on the wall. He touched his wife's arm and looked at her, bringing her attention to the pictures.

She was further saddened by the sight, so she turned her attention to Natasha, who had begun to squirm and whimper.

"We are at your grandparents' house, Tasha. Don't cry. Don t be naughty," Shukri said to the baby gently, his love for his child shining in his eyes.

Laura could not find any rope to hang a sarong for a baby hammock, so she held the baby in her arms and rocked her gently.

"Sis! You're home!" Jenny screamed with joy from the compound. Then she bounded up the stairs and walked into the living room. She hugged Laura hard, making the baby whimper as she felt the squeeze.

Laura was informed that their parents were at Odu Madilin's place. She tensely asked Jenny if their parents knew that she had returned.

Jenny nodded, looking into her sister's face.

"What did they say?" she asked.

"Nothing. They didn't say you shouldn't have come home or anything like that. They just say you should not come to Grandmother's house for the wake and the funeral," Jenny answered.

They either don't care or are no longer angry with me, Laura thought, sighing deeply. She was ready for whatever could happen now that she was home at last.

"Why can't I go to Grandmother's house? Mother doesn't want me to go?" Laura asked Jenny after a pause. She was worried about the implication of this request.

"Nothing like that. You have just given birth, so you are not supposed to attend wakes or funerals. It's taboo," Jenny said.

Mother still cares for me, Laura thought, swallowing hard. She teared up a little and smiled at her younger sister.

"Mother said you must stay home with the baby. If Shukri wants to go, he may come with me," Jenny said, smiling at her handsome brother-in-law.

"Jenny, bring me a rope to make a baby hammock," Laura called out as her sister and Shukri went down the steps.

Jenny turned back, went into another room, and emerged with a clean length of rope, which she gave to Laura. Laura then tied her sarong and tied the rope to the house beam, making a presentable baby hammock for Natasha, who seemed to drift from one sleeping place to another without complaint.

Shukri had wanted to help, but he did not have a chance, as both young women were adept at what they were doing.

"It's done. You can sit down and rest," Jenny said, looking at the hammock and staring at the baby, her niece.

"I will rock you to sleep," Jenny said to Natasha, who looked at her aunt and around the house in wonder.

Jenny took the baby in her arms and rocked her, watched by the mother and father, who were both smiling in amusement.

"You don't need air conditioning, baby. It's cold in here," Jenny said.

"Jenny, get me a match," said Inai Ulis, breaking the atmosphere and startling the three young adults in the house.

Jenny ran over with a match and gave it to her mother. Inai Ulis set fire to a mound of old newspapers and stepped over it. It was a tradition for people to do this after visiting the house of a deceased person.

Jenny also brought her mother a change of clothes and a bath towel. It was also a cultural custom for the people to take a shower and change their clothes after such visits.

Laura, Jenny, and Shukri sat in the living room looking at the baby, who was quietly looking around her.

"Have you been here long?" Inai Ulis spoke, startling the trio. Shukri came forward to hold his mother-in-law's hands and touch them to his forehead.

"We just arrived, Mother," Laura said, hugging her mother, who pulled away after a while to approach the wide-awake beautiful baby girl.

"She looks like you, Laura," Inai Ulis said softly, caressing the baby's fine hair.

"Where's Father?" asked Shukri, daring himself to speak to his mother-in-law, who had yet to look him in the face.

"At your grandmother's place. It will be a busy day today, as they are slaughtering the buffalo," she answered.

"Mother, I would like to go to Grandmother's home and look at her for the last time," Laura said to her mother.

Inai Ulis paused and stared at Laura.

"All right, Laura. Jenny, you keep an eye on the baby. You can't take her to the house of the deceased," she said, fussing with her headcover.

"Okay. Sis, I will take care of the baby. You go and see Grandmother," Jenny said, placing the baby in the hammock and rocking her gently.

Shukri and Laura walked on the meandering pathway towards Odu Madilin's house, trying to catch up with Inai Ulis.

The funereal sounds of the gong echoed in the quaint hamlet, once again announcing the passing of a beloved resident. Laura and Shukri kept walking, sometimes meeting people who were going home from the deceased's house. Some shook hands with the couple, while others nodded their hello.

Shukri and Laura's arrival at Odu Madilin's home was received with cries and lamentation, as most of the relatives knew how close Laura had been to her grandmother.

Her aunts hugged Laura, shedding tears, as she too began to cry for her beloved grandmother. The old lady, who had done a lot for Laura in the past, had been gentle and firm with the children when imparting traditional knowledge.

Laura and Shukri paid their respects to the deceased, both lost in their own thoughts. The old woman looked peaceful as she lay in her coffin.

Shukri later went to the house compound to look for his father-in-law. Laura watched as he mingled with the people, shaking hands and speaking to them. Noticing that her father did not take Shukri's hand, she cried a little.

My poor husband. You try so hard, she thought, feeling proud that Shukri had not let his father-in-law's cool reception deter him. Instead, he mingled with the village folks.

"Mother, forgive me," Laura whispered to her mother, as she sat down next to the elderly woman. Her mother did not answer her. Laura held her mother's hands, looking at her beseechingly.

"That's enough, Laura. We will concentrate on your grandmother's funeral, which will be tomorrow. You should stay at our house until your confinement is over," Inai Ulis said.

Laura bowed her head, but she felt a ray of hope that she would be taken back into the fold.

"Don't stay too long here, Laura. You are still in confinement. Go home now, and take Shukri with you. We will stay here for the wake."

Laura nodded at her mother and then walked down the steps, looking for her father amid the crowd. She saw him speaking to a few people, his drink forgotten. Once she reached him, she held his hands, touching them with her forehead as tears fell from her eyes.

"Father, forgive me," she said, choked with tears.

Her father gently placed his hands on her head and looked into her eyes. His sorrow was written on his face, his eyes filled with pain, but he could not say anything.

"Your grandmother is gone, Laura," were the only words he could muster as he swallowed. His eyes began to water.

Laura watched him, and within her she wanted to believe that his tears were for her too, a ray of hope and happiness at his daughter's return, and with it, forgiveness.

"Father, I will go home now. My baby might cry," she said, taking her leave. She knew she did not sound too convincing, but she didn't want to prolong the atmosphere charged with sadness and regret in that place of mourning.

"Okay, Laura."

She heard her father's voice but didn't attempt to look at him. The charged atmosphere was more than she could bear. She didn't want to end up bawling her eyes out for other reasons than mourning her grandmother.

"You go back, Laura. I will stay a while and help where I can," Shukri told her after she was once again with him. He kissed her forehead. She started to walk briskly home.

"Wait up!"

She turned to look at Shukri, who was running towards her. She stood there waiting until he reached her.

"I will accompany you home, sweetheart, and then I'll return here to help out, where I can of course."

She nodded and reached for his hand. They walked home together in silence, both lost in their own thoughts, yet united through the firm grasp of their hands.

At Laura's parents' house, Shukri gave his wife a kiss and then left her there.

His parting remarks, "Don't touch the baby immediately when you go in," made her smile. He was starting to subscribe to her beliefs. She watched him walk away briskly, and once again she had a sense of pride for her husband.

Chapter 16

It was the third day since Odu Madilin's death, time to bury her. On that day, Shukri woke up to realise that he had been sleeping for two nights at the house of the deceased. It had also been three days since he had seen his baby.

On the third day, he went with the villagers concerned to dig the grave for the deceased. He had been easy-going with the village folks; the men had started to like him. He was friendly and did not turn up his nose when asked to do hard work.

"Your son-in-law is all right, Mikol. He is not fazed by challenging dirty work," one of the men said to Mamai Mikol as they watched Shukri help with the cooking.

Shukri looked comfortable among the villagers, who were speaking in a language that he did not understand. He responded with smiles and nods to them, guessing at what they meant by observing their body language.

"Let's eat," said one of Laura's uncles. Shukri responded with a smile and a gesture, in agreement with the invitation.

Shukri ate with the people at the deceased's house, taking his white rice plain, as eating the meat was not permitted by sharia law. He did not want to offend the people, so he did take a piece of meat and put it on his plate.

"It is our tradition to slaughter a buffalo, a pig, or a chicken to honour the dead, as well as to serve it as food for visitors and the family during the three-day wake," Laura's uncle said, adding that for three days there must be someone awake and keeping vigil in the house of the deceased.

Shukri nodded his understanding of this norm, watching some villagers who were drinking.

"Don't be surprised with the drinking. It is not to express joy for the dead but to serve as a commemoration of her life," the older man said, watching Shukri, who was still watching the drinking session.

Shukri also saw several people who were attired modestly in garb that identified them as Muslims. They mingled with the other guests without any qualms, eating the food without any reservation. At that instance, Shukri felt not only humble but also proud of the followers of his religion.

*   *   *

Shukri went with the funeral procession, which started at the deceased's house, ending at the graveyard. A group of young men carried the gongs and beat them along the way. At times they yelled out the traditional pangki that made Shukri break out in goosebumps. The war cry was to deter evil spirits from disturbing the deceased by possessing her body.

A few elderly men chanted mantras to keep away evil spirits along the way. Shukri, startled by a gunshot, quickly turned to see who had fired the gun. He saw his father-in-law holding his hunting rifle, and for a brief moment he could almost see the handsome man Mikol had been in his younger days, judging by his regal stance.

Upon reaching the graveyard, Shukri watched a man reciting mantras near the open grave and gently hitting the ground with a banana frond. He had so many questions, but he had no one to ask, as Laura was not with him. His mother-in-law had strictly forbidden him to bring her along.

"Don t bring your wife along with you for the funeral, as she is still under confinement. It's taboo for her to attend a funeral," Inai Ulis had stated.

Shukri had nodded in assent, listening closely to his mother-in-law.

Laura had approached him earlier and told him that she wanted to see her grandmother for the last time and later join the funeral procession to the graveyard. He was quite reluctant to bring her along, as he didn't like to see her cry.

Inai Ulis had said to Shukri, "Women in confinement are not allowed to go to a wake or a funeral, as they are still fragile physically and spiritually. Laura was allowed to see her grandmother when she first arrived, as she is a close relative, but otherwise it's not allowed."

After the funeral, Shukri returned to the deceased's house with the people. His job was to carry all the tools that had been used to dig the grave and to close it.

"All these implements have to be cleaned before returning them to the respective owners. Of course we can't just return them; we have to pay sogit to the owners," Laura's uncle told Shukri as they cleaned the hoes and spades.

"What will be given to them, Uncle?" Shukri asked, tying his bundle of tools together with a rope.

"It could be chicken or money or both," the older man said, gathering up the tools he had cleaned and setting them aside.

Clapping Shukri on the back, the older man smiled. "Members of the family will gather in the house of the deceased for seven days, not allowing it to be empty. On the seventh day, a feast will be held, and then everyone can go home," he said.

Shukri nodded and then followed the man to the house compound, He was glad that he had taken a week's leave from his job. He was actually quite interested in learning the culture and tradition of his wife's village, but he was also hoping that his stay in the village would somehow bridge the divide between him and his in-laws.

He approached his father-in-law. The two men stared at one another.

"Father, I am going home now. I haven't seen my baby for three days," he said, reaching out to the elderly man. He felt that Mamai Mikol would not answer him.

"Hmm … remember not to immediately go into the house when you reach home," Mamai Mikol answered, looking away.

Shukri felt a leap of joy in his heart. The old man was not angry with him anymore!

"Thank God!" Shukri whispered. Then he briskly walked home. He was very happy that his father-in-law had deigned to speak to him, as it augured well for his future relationship with his in-laws.

Upon reaching home, he called out to his sister-in-law. The young woman looked out through the window to grin at him. "Hold on, I am coming down with matches and a changes of clothes," she said, smiling at him.

Laura looked out too and smiled at her husband. "Tired?"

"Not at all. It was informative," Shukri said, smiling and reaching out for the clothes and matches that Jenny held out.

After stepping over the burning mound of newspapers, taking a shower, and changing his clothes, Shukri walked up to the house, smelling fresh. He sat down near Laura, and reached out to hold Natasha in his arms.

"I miss my pretty Huminodun," he said, holding his baby close.

"Did you drink?" Laura asked.

"Alcohol? No. The smell makes me dizzy as it is," Shukri answered.

"I don't like you to drink," Laura said.

"If I drink with you, it's all right, but only with you." Her husband laughed.

"Sis, Father is coming home," Jenny said, whispering to Laura.

Mamai Mikol entered.

Shukri smiled. Laura held his hands hard. She was almost shivering with fear. She didn't know what to expect at that moment.

"Where is Mother?" Jenny asked her father, looking around.

"She was walking behind me. She will be home shortly," her father answered. His voice was as firm and steely as it had always been. Laura sat there mesmerised, like a child who had done something really bad.

Suddenly Natasha gave a cry that startled her parents and those around her. Shukri thought that the baby was afraid of her grandfather.

"The baby is crying. She must be hungry," Mamai Mikol said as he went into the kitchen. A few minutes later, he appeared in a change of clothes and started out for the compound of the house.

"Jenny, you stay with your sister at home," the older man added.

Shukri was quite jubilant, as it seemed his in-laws were ready to make peace with him and the situation at hand. If they hadn't accepted him, then he and his wife and daughter would have been shouted out of the house by then.

"Did you talk to Father while you were at Grandmother's house?" Laura asked her husband, her eyes searching his face.

"I did try, but he ignored me," he answered, smiling at her.

Laura sighed.

"It's all right, dear. We will just persevere. As long as they don't throw us out," he said.

Laura nodded.

"It seems I may have to be at Grandmother's house for the next seven days, according to tradition," Shukri said, looking out of the window and watching his father-in-law, who was briskly walking towards his deceased mother's house.

"I didn't hear him invite you."

"Your uncle told me that we have to keep vigil at the house until the seventh day," Shukri said, stressing the point.

"That's for the immediate family, dear, and the in-laws."

"I am an in-law," Shukri stressed, holding Laura's shoulders and looking into her face.

Laura laughed a little laugh and teased him about being a West Malaysian who was becoming a Sabahan. They held each other for a while, thinking of all their challenges, and the strength of their love surmounting all odds.

"Sis, I am going to sleep at Grandmother's house today with our aunts," Jenny said.

"I will be alone in the house then. I don't think I dare to be alone," Laura said, looking at her sister beseechingly.

"Shukri can stay home with you. You don't need to go, Shukri," Jenny said, grinning at her brother-in-law.

Shukri smiled at Jenny and nodded.

"That's a good idea. I think you should go now before it gets too dark," the tall young man said, looking at his diminutive sister-in-law.

Laura nodded in agreement, saying that Jenny would not be able to see the path if it got too dark.

Jenny laughed and said she would be careful. Laura looked out through the doorway as her sister walked into the gathering dusk.

"Tell them Shukri can't be there because he is staying with me in the house," Laura called out. "Take care! Be careful," she added.

"Okay! I will do that!" Jenny called back, walking briskly towards her deceased grandmother's home.

"Natasha seems to love it here. Look at her; she sleeps so well. After taking her milk, she goes back to sleep." Laura gazed at her daughter, her face full of love.

"Well, she loves it because it's fresh and cool here, as if the place has natural air conditioning. Twenty-four hours of cool, comfortable air," Shukri answered, touching the baby's face. The baby slept on, oblivious to her surroundings.

Shukri looked at his wife and took her hands, entwining his wide fingers with her slender ones.

"Laura, I will finish my annual leave of two weeks here in the village. I believe you should stay here until the end of your maternity leave. You can return to KL after that," he said, watching Laura's face.

"Do you agree with that, Laura?" Shukri asked, as Laura looked at him in silence.

"I would love to do that. I can spend more time with my parents. You don't mind, do you?" Laura answered.

"Actually, I want you to be with me in KL. I don't really want you to be so far away here," he said thoughtfully.

Laura stared at him.

"What I want, actually, is for you to stay here and be with your family so that the love and affinity you had with them will be as it was. They might be more accepting of us. I honestly just want them to forgive us and accept us as we are.

"I believe that prosperity and happiness will ensue when they forgive us and bless our marriage," Shukri elaborated, his thoughts going back to the year when they were first married.

"You are sure you want me to stay behind?" Laura asked.

"Yes, dear, I am sure. You have two more months to go," her husband answered. "I won't be too long away. I will ask for an unpaid leave so that I can return and spend more time here. I think I should be back here before you finish your leave."

Laura looked at Shukri, her eyes brimming with happiness. Her husband was so understanding and accommodating that she almost couldn't believe it.

"Don't play the field while I am away though," Laura said, half-joking.

"You! Such things never cross my mind, dear one." Shukri looked into his beautiful wife's face.

Laura laughed and kissed her husband's hands. They held each other for a while, each one lost in their own thoughts.

Shukri thought of his experience during the two nights' wake he had carried out at Laura's grandmother's ceremony for the dead. He did not sleep well, as there were always people who were awake and chatting the night away. However, he had learned a lot about his wife's culture, the taboos and the ceremonies. It was strange to him, almost exotic, but he understood the implications of each ceremony. Besides that, Laura's aunts and cousins had been friendly and quite pleasant with him.

"You should move to Kota Kinabalu, Shukri. Get a job here," one of Laura's aunts had said to him.

"I would love to, but I am worried about my mother. She is old and lives alone at home," he had said, sharing his thoughts with his rapt audience.

"That's not a problem. You could bring her here to live with you. You won't have to worry anymore," the elderly woman had answered.

Shukri thought about the suggestion long and hard, and he began to like the idea. *It might be a very good idea,* he thought, his eyes growing heavy.

Before peaceful sleep embraced him, he thought about his mother. He planned his future life to ensure that his family, the one in Johor and the one in Kota Kinabalu, would stay together in peace and harmony.

Glossary

Inai	Aunt; a term of respect
Mamai	Uncle; a term of respect
pangki	war cry
seruling	flute
siung	conical hat
timbok	head ornament for keeping hair up
tongkungon	musical instrument made of bamboo
sogit	conciliatory fine or a payment for certain matters
Sumazau	A traditional Kadazandusun (ethnic) dance
Kulintangan	A series of small gongs place on a bamboo bracket container. They usually placed on the ground anfd played by hitting them in certain sequence.
Sirung	A conical head gear used by village women (Native of Kadazandusun)
Sompoton	A musical instrument made from bamboo and dried gourd.
Huminodun	A deity daughter of god called Kinoringan and goddess Suminundu. She was sacrifice during a famine where her body was chopped up and scattered on a cultivation area which become food plant.